Dedicati

For many, many reasons, this novel is very special to me. It is closer to my heart than any other work I've ever written. I need to dedicate this novel to my daughters, Breathe and Alight. They teach me anew, every day, how to experience life joyfully, as God intended for us all to do.

I thank Breathe, especially, for always making me laugh and for her pure sweetness. She is the most thoughtful and intelligent five year old I have ever encountered. Her trust in God is astounding, and inspiring. I deeply love how imaginative she is, and how much she thrives off of pretend play. The memories we've created of playing horses and babies and Elephants in the Jungle are more precious to me than anything else I have.

I thank Alight, particularly for her sense of independence and her sense of adventure. It delights my heart to see her love of books and it thrills me to experience the wonder and magic of all the neat places in our city with her. She makes going outside an exciting thing to do. She is only three, and yet her very presence lights up my life. I am eternally grateful for dinosaurs, cars, purses and little toys because, when Alight sees them, she smiles and when she smiles, so does my heart. When I was a little girl, I used to dream about becoming someone just like Alight.

These two little girls delight my soul, rejuvenate my weary heart and remind me of God's light. The greatest gift of my life is being able to witness the both of you grow into happy, healthy, secure, confident girls who obviously love life. Thank you for all the moments and all the memories

that you have given me.
I am deeply in love with you both.

Love, Mommy

Though the plight of abused children is a reality faced by every nation in the world, this particular novel, with its cast of characters and events, is a work of fiction.

If, however, you are a survivor of any type of childhood trauma, many things in this novel could act as triggers.

Please make sure you are safe before reading.

Prologue:
The Only One

There is something really, really important about me that you should know right away. The thing is, it's kind of a secret. I have lots of them. I always have. I probably always will. Sometimes, it's even a secret from me. If I don't think about it too much, sometimes I don't even remember this one secret myself. But today, there was this cop that came to my school. She was talking to us about how important it is to stay in school. Like we have a choice or something. Anyway, the first thing she did was make everybody introduce themselves. She said she wanted us to tell her something about ourselves that she wouldn't know just by looking at us. That's what reminded me of this one secret. I didn't tell her the secret, though, cause I didn't want to. It makes me sound like a real loser. But I'll tell it to you. Here it is: I only have one memory of my dad that is good. Just one. I have memories of stuff he's bought me, and of things he did for me, but something bad usually always comes with something good. At least, it does for my dad and me. Except one time. It happened just a few days before he went away.

It was a really nice day. Daddy said it would be a shame if we didn't get out and enjoy the weather. He said that we should go swimming at the lake. My mom worked the night before, though. She was tired and so she didn't want to come. I didn't really want to go if Mama wasn't coming. I always get a little nervous and a little bit scared if it's just me and Daddy. But I'm only ten. I couldn't say no. And, besides, I really love to swim.

I put my feet on the back of the front seat while Daddy was driving. It was comfortable. I thought he'd tell me to take my feet down, but he didn't. He also let me choose what CD we listened to. I started getting happier about coming swimming as we were driving. I could tell that Daddy was in a good mood. When we got to the lake, though, and I saw that there weren't a lot of people there, I got nervous again. I was going to have to get in the pool with just my bathing suit on. That's kind of like being naked. And I really, really don't like to be naked. Being naked reminds me of another secret.

Daddy was real happy, though. He laid out our towel not too far from the water. He told me that he was going swimming and I could, too, if I wanted, or I could just sit and watch. He said I'd have to be really silly not to get in the water. I still couldn't get past the idea of taking off my shirt and shorts. I don't understand why you have to be in a bathing suit to get in the water: why can't you wear even just a t-shirt?

I sat down on the towel and watched the few people swimming. Daddy was diving under the water and then swimming a little bit away from the shore. There were two girls, a little bit younger than me, playing. They kept splashing each other and laughing. Their mom sat on a towel watching them, and I thought it was weird how she let them get in the water by themselves when they were younger than me. I'm ten and I know how to swim, and still my mom only lets me do that when she's in a really, really good mood.

Daddy held up one arm and waved me in.

"Come on, Anna, don't be such a baby! The water feels great! You're missing all the fun!"

The water did look fun.

I love the water.

I just didn't want to be naked.

But no one was watching. I kept telling myself that I would have the bathing suit on, that I wasn't really naked. I was really hot, too. The sun was right over my head, and I just knew that I was getting burned. The water would cool me off. There were other people here. That meant that I was probably safe. Daddy probably wouldn't do anything as long as there were other people around. He never did anything when Mama was home.

I looked to see if anyone was looking at me. I looked to see if Daddy was looking at me, but he was underwater again. I looked one more time to make sure that no one else was looking at me. Then I took my t-shirt off and undid my shorts. I managed to get out of them without having to stand up. Then I just took a deep, deep breath, pushed myself to my hands and stood. Then I took off.

I don't like to wait around. It is worse for me to "ease my way in" as Mama does. It's better if I just get it over with. I'm like that with a lot of other things, too. Anyway, so I didn't just stick my foot or toe in: I ran as far out into the water as I could, and then I went under. All at once. The water rushed over my face and then soaked my hair, making it all heavy and dark. The water was cool but it felt good.

All of a sudden, something splashed me in the back.

I turned around and Daddy was grinning. He had splashed me! I didn't know what to do but he was smiling, and I remembered seeing the other girls splash each other. So I splashed him back. He started laughing.

"Bet you can't get me now!" he called and took off swimming.

I splashed as hard as I could. The water went everywhere.

Then Daddy dove underwater. It wasn't real clear, and I lost sight of him. The next thing I knew, something had me by the ankles. I only had a second to figure that out before I was jerked under the water. Luckily, I grabbed my nose and closed my eyes a second before the water rushed up my face. When I came back up, Daddy was still laughing.

"Got you. Now, it's your turn to try and dunk me."

I wasn't sure about this. This could so easily turn out really bad for me. But he was laughing. He didn't seem serious, like he did when something bad was going to happen. And if I told him that I didn't want to play, he'd get mad. So I started swimming after him. I knew I wouldn't be able to chase him, but swimming was fun. I liked the way my arms pushed the water out of my way every time they hit the water in a stroke. Swimming hard and pushing my legs real hard made me feel like I was doing something. It made me feel kind of like I was free.

Me and Daddy splashed each other for a long time.

Then he said, "Do you want me to throw you from my shoulders? It's real fun."

Daddy is hard to say no to.

Besides, I didn't really like saying it, but I was

having fun. The reason I didn't like saying it was cause I don't really like saying that any time with Daddy was fun. It makes me feel…well, just…bad. Like I'm a bad person or something. But I was having fun. I could feel my heart beating real fast, and a couple of times I even laughed out loud—when I got to splash him or he let me push him under the water. One time, when he popped back up, he tipped his head way back to the sky and squirted out a beam of water in the air. He said he was a whale. That was funny, so I laughed. My grandma once said that no one could meet my dad and not like him. When he's being nice, that's about right.

He bent down and helped me get on his shoulders. He had to hold my ankles, but he just held my ankles and then he told me to stand up. On top of his shoulders! I was real nervous about that, cause I thought I might fall or something and get hurt. But it was kind of exciting, too. And cool. So he took my hands and I did it: I stood up on his shoulders. Then he told me to jump off, over his head, when he counted to three.

I hit the water hard, but it didn't hurt. When I came up, I was smiling. He was too.

"Like that?" he asked.

"Again," I said.

He laughed.

***** ***** *****

When we got out of the water, Daddy said he had a surprise for me. He told me to wait on the towel. He went back to the car and he came back with Mama's picnic basket. It was wicker and it was real big. I loved Mama's picnic basket. Daddy said he thought we might get hungry, so he'd packed us a lunch.

I was glad: I was really hungry. And he packed my favorite sandwich: peanut butter and honey. He also packed my favorite kind of chips: Doritos. He even packed me an apple and a Coke, too. We didn't have ice, but that was okay. It was still cold from when it'd been in the fridge at home. Daddy and me sat on the towel and ate our lunch. We didn't talk a whole lot, but that was okay. I started to take a bite out of my peanut butter and honey sandwich when I saw this little girl and her dad trying to find a spot to put down their towels. They were just getting to the lake. They were holding hands. Usually, whenever I saw kids with their dads, I got sad. But I wasn't sad then. In fact, I felt almost just like that little girl.

It was a good day. I was so glad that I went swimming with him. I'm even more glad about it now, though. If I had stayed home instead, I wouldn't have one single good memory of Daddy.

1

Memories

"They call it 'balls.' You know, they'll say things like 'You've got no balls, man.' Well, my sister says that's what they're talking about: their, you know…"

"No way."

"You mean they have two of them? I thought it was just one."

"There's just one that gets, you know, hard. I think. I don't know. But all guys have two of them."

"What's the other one for?"

"I don't know. She didn't tell me that."

"What I don't get is why they call them balls. I mean, it's not round, it's long, right?"

"That is so weird."

"How does your sister know all this anyway? I don't think it's right. I think she was making it up."

"No. She's, you know, *done* it."

"No way."

"Way. She's seventeen."

"You'll have to ask her some more questions then."

"For real."

They finally leave.

They were dressed a long time ago and were still hanging around so they could talk about the hard thing. I felt really sick to my stomach. I swear, they are like aliens to me. Girls, I mean. I know I'm a girl, too, but whenever I'm around other girls, I sure don't feel like one. I feel more like an ant than a girl. They talk about boys and the hard thing as if it's a good thing. I bet that girl's sister wouldn't call it a good thing—not if she really has *done* it. They talk

12

about it as though they'd be happy to see one in real life. I bet they would laugh if a boy pulled his pants down.

Not me.

Hearing them talk about it makes me feel, well, like I said, like a bug. I'm not normal. I don't feel things that girls are supposed to feel. Not only about this sort of stuff, but other stuff, too. Like, the girls in my class, most of them care a lot about what they wear. Not me. I could wear the same thing five days in a row and be perfectly fine. I probably would, if I could get past my mother.

I stuffed my foot into my teeny shoe, grabbed my book bag, and headed out of the locker room. It was time for class again. 'Cept, even as I was walking to class, I kept thinking about what the girls were talking about. I walked into class, and I sat down at the desk that's closest to the door. Sometimes this desk is already taken when I get back from the locker room, but not today. I am glad. I like sitting next to the door.

In my head, I saw a picture of Daddy.

I took my pencil out and opened up the story notebook. I didn't really know what to write, though. So I started doodling. Then I remembered that I'd never written it down. I still had a few minutes before Mrs. Keller started class. I bend my head and start writing.

***** ***** *****

I was seven.

And I remember.

Some people say that you forget stuff that happened to you when you were a little kid. Mama says that she don't remember nothing before she was about eleven. I guess that's just another way that I'm different than all the other girls. Maybe that's why they seem like aliens to me. Or maybe I'm the alien.

13

Anyway, about forgetting.

*Daddy said I would. Forget, that is. That first time,
he said I'd forget. But that was three years ago, and I ain't
forgot. Maybe I have to grow up first. Maybe that's the
trick. When you grow up, maybe you forget about stuff that
happened when you was little. I don't know what I think
about that. It might be nice. To forget. Sometimes I wonder
what it would feel like to wake up and not remember. But,
it's kind of scary, too. I don't really want to forget. I mean,
what if I forgot and then it happened to me again the same
day I forgot? That would mean I'd have to be as scared as I
was the first time all over again. That would mean I'd have
to freak out all over again. I think I like it better the way it
is now: at least I know about it all. At least I don't get as
scared as I did then. At least it's normal.*

*It was a rainy day, that day I learned about the hard
thing. It was also my first day as a second grade student. It
was a big day. All I remember about that day at school was
the dress I wore. It was white with red daisies all over it.
There is a picture of me standing in front of the school,
wearing that dress, and holding my lunchbox, that Mama
took. I remember her giving me a big hug before she took
the picturse and another big hug after she took the picture.
I don't like looking at that picture cause it hurts. I looked
happy. I had bangs then. They were short. The rest of my
hair hung down straight as a board behind my back. I
looked like a good kid. That's why looking at the picture
hurts. I looked like a good kid. I've always wanted to be a
good kid. I looked even a little bit normal. I've always
wanted to be normal, too. The thing is, I'm not good, and
I'm not normal. At least not anymore.*

*There were two girls in my class. One was named
Amanda and the other Rain. When we went out to play on
the playground that day, they both wanted to play with me.
I was sitting on the swings and I remember feeling happy. I*

14

was happy cause Rain and Amanda wanted to play with me. They wanted to play different things, though. They started getting angry at each other and I felt proud. They were fighting over me. I am ten now, and that's never happened to me since. No one ever wants to play with me now. But they did then. Before I changed. Before I got bad. Amanda is still in my class now but she isn't my friend anymore. I don't know why. She just kind of stopped playing with me. Or maybe I stopped playing with her. I don't remember anymore. All I know is that we don't talk or hang out on the playground like we did in second grade. Rain moved to a different school. I don't even know where she is anymore. If Mama's right about how you forget stuff as you grow, then she probably don't even remember me anymore. But I remember her. She was one of the only people who ever wanted to play with me.

That's what I told Mama about when I got home. I told her about playing on the playground with Rain and Amanda. I told her how much fun that was. She said that she was glad that I had some friends. Daddy said he was, too. He wanted me to come sit with him and tell him about school while Mama cooked dinner. I was happy, so I did. I sat down in front of him in the living room. That's when he started playing with my hair. It didn't bother me. It didn't hurt, either. And I didn't feel bad. He was just playing with my hair. He said it was soft. He said it was pretty. That made me happy, too.

"Anna? Anna, are you paying attention? You need to get out your Social Studies book now."

Mrs. Keller was looking at me funny. I stopped writing and lifted my head. I remembered now that I was in school, but not the second grade. I was back in my regular classroom. I was supposed to be listening to the lesson. She might ask me a question if she thought I wasn't paying attention. I shut the story notebook and reached into my desk. I pulled out the Social Studies workbook really fast, mumbling about how sorry I was. Mrs. Keller nodded and left me alone. My face was hot. I was really embarrassed. I hated being called out by the teacher. I hated the teacher talking to me at all in school. Being an ant for real wouldn't be that bad in class. No one would be able to see me.

I looked down at the workbook. I tried to listen. I really, really did. But all I could think about was the first day of second grade.

***** ***** *****

I was too worried that I would get in trouble again if I opened the story notebook. Mrs. Keller might even ask to see what I was writing. That would be horrible. So I didn't write any more about what I remembered at school. I walked home. Mama was in the kitchen. I like helping Mama cook. She asked me about my day.

"Did you have a test today?"

I shook my head.

"No. Tomorrow we have one."

"I'll help you study if you want, after dinner."

I shrugged.

"Okay."

"Here. Why don't you wash these potatoes for me?"

Mama handed me the pot of potatoes, and I took them over to the sink. They were heavy. I was happy she was going to make fried potatoes. They were my favorite.

My mom and I are friends. That's something else that's different about me and the other girls in my class. Most of them talk about their moms as though they are always being told what to do and getting in trouble for not doing it. Mama doesn't tell me not to do much. And when she does tell me to do something, I always do it right away. It's about the only thing I am good at: obeying. I wish I looked more like her. She has this really pretty hair that comes down really long and these big eyes. Her skin is tanned, too. Me, I look like a ghost. The doctor says I don't have enough iron, so Mama is always cooking stuff that has lots of iron in it. She even packs raisin boxes in my lunches for school.

I started to relax a little. I liked being home. I liked cooking. The potatoes were all washed now. I asked her if I could help her cut them, too.

"Hm. Okay. But you have to be careful—it's a sharp knife."

She gave me the knife, and I started to cut up the potatoes. There is something about cooking. I like how you take something that's raw and you turn it into something that you can eat. I also like all the work. I like cutting and washing. I like stirring and measuring and mixing. And I really like boiling water. I think it's really neat how bubbles start coming up out of the water when it gets hot. Sometimes, when I'm home by myself, I will put a pot of water on the stove and make it boil—just to watch it boil. When the bubbles get so big that it starts spilling over the sides of the pot, I fix it, but I think that part is cool. It reminds me of me. Sometimes it feels like there's lots of bubbles under my skin. I know that one day the bubbles are going to burst out of me. I wonder what will happen then. Mama says that it makes her nervous. She knows I like watching the water boil so she won't let me do it. She says that one day, I'm not going to be paying enough attention and I'm going to get burned by the water.

"Okay, kiddo, I think I can handle it from here. You can just go play for a while before supper. Do your homework."

I handed her the last of the cut-up potatoes and headed out of the kitchen.

I walked through the living room where Daddy is sitting on the couch. He is reading the paper, and he has the TV turned on the news channel.

"Hey, peaches. Just saw the weather report. It's going to be a little cool tomorrow. When you put out your clothes for school tonight, keep that in mind."

"Yes, sir."

I kept walking.

"Hey, Anna?"

I stopped.

"I like your hair. It's cute in pigtails like that."

"Thank you."

But my teeth were ground together and my voice was soft.

I just wanted to get to my room now.

As soon as I did, I grabbed the story notebook and sat down on the floor, with my back leaning against the bed. I really wanted to write down all of what I remembered. It was the only way to get it out of my head.

***** ***** *****

Mama is a nurse. She just started being one. She was real excited when she got the piece of paper that said she could work in a hospital. She works at night and I stay at home with Daddy. Sometimes Daddy plays games with me. He's real good at being the Tickle Monster. He likes to play that game. Sometimes he'll grab me around my waist and pull me down. He thinks it's funny. I don't really like it as much as he does, but it's okay. I do like making him happy. He played that game with me tonight. I didn't want to go to bed so I asked him if he could chase me around the house. He said no, that big girls have to go to bed. Then he said something funny. He said, "Did you know that going to bed can be fun?"

18

I didn't know that.

He nodded and his eyes got real big.

"It's a game. And it's real fun. Grown-ups play it all the time. But...I don't know if you're old enough. You know what, maybe we should just wait until you're bigger."

"No! I'm big enough. I'm in the second grade. Show me the game!"

"Well..."

He put his hand on his chin, like he was thinking about it. Sometimes that meant he'd let me do what I want. Sometimes it meant he wouldn't. I wished I could have figured out which one it was now. I really wanted to play the game. I didn't believe that bedtime could be fun. Finally, he put his hands on his hips.

"Alright. But here's the thing. It's real, real important. Mamas don't like little girls playing this game. It makes them get mad if they find out because they want little girls to be asleep. Do you want to go to sleep?"

I shook my head.

"No."

"Then you have to promise you won't tell your mama about the game. She'll get mad and bedtime won't be fun anymore."

"Okay. I won't tell."

"That's my girl. You're such a special girl. Go on to your room and put on your gown."

"But—"

I thought he was going to make me go to bed.

"Just do it. It's part of the fun."

"Okay."

So I went to my room. Mama always put out my gown for me before she left for work. She lays it on my bed. Tonight, she left the red gown with the white hearts on it. I like it. It has long sleeves so I stay warm when I wear it. I put it on. I started to walk out of my room to go find Daddy,

19

but before I could he opened the door. He looked funny—he wasn't wearing a shirt. I started laughing. Daddy was always supposed to wear a shirt.

"Oh, it's funny, huh?"

He leaned down and picked me up. He took me to the bed and dropped me on it. But he got on the bed, too, and laid down beside me. Then he moved his hand down and under my gown. My smile dropped a little. I didn't understand. He moved his hand up until he touched my chest.

"You are really soft. I'm proud of you for being ready for the big girl game," he said.

When I felt him touch my star panties, I tried to move away from him but he held me so I couldn't move.

"You gotta be still."

Then he took his hand away and I felt better. I started to sit up, but he shook his head and told me to stay laid down. So I did.

"I—I don't want to play this game."

"Oh, sure you do. You just be still."

He took off his pants and his underwear.

I felt really nervous now. I wasn't sure at all about this. Mama says I'm not allowed to go into the bathroom if a grown-up is in one. She says I'm not allowed to come in her room if she or Daddy isn't dressed. I didn't think I was supposed to see Daddy without clothes on. And his hand was hurting me. I just wanted it to stop. It wasn't a game anymore. I just wanted to go to sleep.

He wanted me to stay still but I couldn't. I kept moving. I was crying, too. He said I was not being a good girl. I didn't have anywhere to put my hands so I put them on his arms. His arms are hairy and big. He was breathing funny now—real hard. I felt it on my face. I tried to turn my head, but there was nothing else to see but him. I was really scared now. I really wanted him to go away. I tried pushing *on him. I asked him to stop, but he didn't. He didn't stop. Then he took one of my hands and pulled it down. It touched something hard, really hard. And big, too. I didn't know what it was. It made me cry even harder. Daddy made a funny sound and the next thing that happened was something sticked me—it sticked me hard, where I pee pee. I screamed, but Daddy took one hand and put it over my mouth. He said something, but I couldn't hear what he said. My head felt really bad now. My body did, too.*

I looked up and saw a crack in the ceiling. It made me cry even more. I think I'd just cracked.

The sticking thing comes out now, and Daddy gets off me. I was shaking real bad. I was still crying, too. I didn't know what had just happened. I was so scared. Daddy leaves the room. I tried to roll over and when I did, I noticed something. Blood. It wasn't a lot of blood, but it was blood. And it was on my legs. I screamed out and started crying real loud. I was hurt. I was bleeding. I was probably going to die now. I wanted my mama. I screamed that out, as loud as I could.

"Mama! I want Mama!"

The door opened. But it wasn't Mama. It was Daddy again.

"Anna, what did I tell you? Mama cannot know about this. She'll get mad at you. If she gets mad at you, I'll have to get on to you. It'll be even worse than this was. This wasn't so bad. You'll forget all about it. But if you aren't a good girl, it will have to get worse. Are you going to make Mama mad?"

I shook my head. I started scooting back cause he was walking up toward the bed. I wished he wouldn't do that. I didn't want him to come to the bed anymore.

"I'm just going to clean you up. That's all."

He had a washcloth in his hand. He put it between my legs. That made me jump. I could feel his hand even though he had the washcloth there.

"It's okay, it's okay," I said.

I just wanted him to leave. He told me to take my gown off and he'd give me a new one. I did, and I cried when I saw that it had blood on it. He gave me a new gown. Then he smiled at me as he watched me put it on.

"You're not a baby anymore, Anna. You're a big girl now. Daddy's girl. You remember that."

It was a long time before I went to sleep.

2
The Introduction

All sound is made from vibrations. When we first learned that in science class at school, I almost laughed out loud. I mean, when I think of something vibrating, I don't think of sound, I think of something shaking. But Mrs. Keller, our teacher, made us put our fingers over our throats and say something. I just said my name but when I did, I could feel my throat vibrating. It was really weird. I went home and started playing with my music stuff, trying to see if it was really true or not. I have this little guitar. It's nothing big or fancy, but it has strings on it and my mom says it's still in tune. So I strummed it a little and when I did, I noticed how the strings were kind of pulled back and then released so that they kind of hit another one. I saw how strumming the strings made it vibrate. I thought that was so cool. I thought about the music I hear on the radio and on my CDs. I thought in one song there must be thousands of vibrations. If a vibration caused noise, how did the musicians control the sound to make it sound like a song? I'm a dork. I walked around most of the day with my fingers on my throat, feeling it vibrate every time I said anything. Then I started thinking about the skating rink and all the music played there. Music that was always so loud. Kids that were loud. Popcorn popping at the concession stand. Skates sliding along the floor. Must be millions of vibrations in such a busy place. It makes sense why when it's real loud my insides start to feel shaken up.

***** ***** *****

The small table sits in the corner of the dark skating rink. On the table my mom has put the four presents. They are wrapped in pretty red wrapping paper. There are red paper plates and napkins, too. The birthday cake is my favorite kind—chocolate with chocolate icing. It has ten candles on it. Daddy has just gone to order a pizza. He is ordering a large one. We won't ever eat all of it. There are lots of people here at the skating rink. There are lots of kids, too, but I don't know any of them. I make sure not to say anything about that to Mama. I just try to get my brown rental skates on as fast as I can. I just want to get out on the skating rink to skate. We almost never come skating.

Mama looks at her watch again. She pushes her hair back off her face and glances towards the front door. She still thinks that a couple of kids from my school might show up. It would make her happy if even one came. It would make me happy, too, but I know it's not going to happen. I stand up. The skates are real tight and I'm a little shaky on them. I put my hand on the table to steady myself. As sort of a test, I push my left foot out a little and then bring it back. I slowly take my hand off the table and try it again. I don't fall, so that's good.

"You going on out?" Mama asks.

I nod.

"Okay, hon."

As I slowly skate towards the rink, I feel like an idiot. I like skating, but I'm not good at it. I am sure there are other kids here looking at me. I am ten today. I should be able to skate. It's okay, though. It is my birthday, and I am going to have fun. I finally reach the rink and step onto the slippery floor. People start whizzing past me. They are going super fast, and the neon lights that are flashing on the floor make it hard to stay focused. I crowd closer to the wall and sort of inch my way along. A little girl, like, way littler than me, skates in front of me and holds onto the wall. She is going about the same pace I am. Watching her in front of me, holding onto the wall, makes me feel even dumber. She's, like, a little kid. I should be able to skate better than her. I wonder if I can pretend that I'm her sister or something and act like I'm helping her learn to skate. Then it wouldn't seem weird that I am going so slow.

Even though it's pretty obvious I stink at it, skating rinks have always been one of my favorite places. I like the energy. I like how there are always cool kids hanging out right alongside the misfits. Daddy brought me to one for the first time when I was, like, seven. I was slipping and sliding all over the place, but he held my hand so I didn't fall all the way down too many times. He said we'd have to make it a habit, going skating together, and when I got real good, he said we'd have races. But before it could ever happen, we'd always have to move. Or Daddy would be on one of his anger streaks and Mama would have to bring me. Mama don't get on the rink. I think she's scared that she'll fall and, you know, break a bone or something. "That would be a mess," she says. "Who would drive you home?" I guess she has a point. Still, even though I haven't really had a lot of time to get good at it, when Mama asked me where I wanted my birthday party to be, I knew it was the rink.

The music can drown everything else out, even my own voice. The music makes me forget all kinds of stuff. Even if it's not music I really like a lot, I still like listening to it when I'm at the rink. Sometimes it's nice to be shaken up inside so that I can't think. Sometimes not thinking is better than knowing everything. Besides, I thought that a few of the kids would want to come skating enough that they might show up, even though it is **my** birthday. I'm really not too smart. I mean, after all, only about three kids at school even know who I am. But me and Mama always try to do that—schedule the birthday party at a place we think kids would like to come. It never works.

I was finally coming back around to where I started. Daddy waved me over. It was time for cake and pizza. I'll get to open presents. I step off the rink and skate towards my parents. The four birthday presents, the cake sitting in front of the pizza, the paper plates, napkins and cups—it was for me. The only people who would sing "happy birthday" to me were my parents. There might be someone here from my school who would see. It was hard to listen to the music or feel excited when I felt like such a baby. I felt my heart drop to my feet. Having a birthday party at a skating rink was a dumb idea.

***** ***** *****

I really like the maple tree in our backyard. It's not like we have a fancy house or anything, cause we don't. It's not like we have a fancy backyard, cause we don't. In fact, that's kind of why I like the maple tree: it is one of the only fancy things I can say for sure we do have. It's really nice to sit under it. I like to read a lot and I like to do it sitting under my maple tree. Right now, I'm reading *The Reluctant Dragon*. The librarian at my school told me it would be good. I wasn't so sure. I mean, it was about a dragon. Maybe I don't play baby dolls and tea parties anymore but I'm not exactly into G.I. Joes and dragons, either. But I didn't know what else to read since I've already gone through the whole list of recommended books for my grade this year. So I got it. And it is pretty good. It's about this dragon who doesn't want to scare kids, or breathe fire or, you know, do any of the dragon-like stuff he's supposed to do. Nobody *gets* this dragon at all. That is something I know all about. The cool part is that, in the book, there's this boy who tries to make the dragon his friend. That's

26

more than I can say about pretty much any of the kids in my class.

Anyway, that's what I came out here to do. Read. I have the book opened and everything but I can't concentrate on it too good. My mind keeps wandering back to the skating rink. It was embarrassing but I am glad that I got to go skating. Daddy actually got on the rink with me after we ate pizza and had cake. A couple of people stopped by to tell me happy birthday, too, when they saw all the party stuff Mama had set up. I liked all my presents.

I give up on reading.

I bet Daddy would let me walk to the park for a while. It's right at the end of our street. I do it all the time, and there's still plenty of time before dark. I really need to do something to help me think about something else.

***** ***** *****

There are tons of kids at the park. You'd think that I would not like this, since I don't have any friends. Actually, though, I like watching kids my age, but only if I don't really know them. If I don't know them, they won't think that my watching them means I want to be like them or anything dumb like that. Cause I don't. Still, it's sort of interesting to see what they talk about and what kinds of games they play. I don't like the same things they do, and it's weird hearing them talk about how they've got crushes on guys or about the latest Harry Potter movie. I've read the books and didn't care enough about it to see the movie. I for real could not talk about Harry Potter for as long as the other girls I know do. But at least watching them and listening to them makes me feel like I know what's going on, anyway. I'm not a complete idiot when someone says something cool to me.

I like the park. It has a pond where about ten ducks
swim. It's very pretty. There are these iron benches that are
so close to the water I can actually feed the ducks and sit at
the same time. Lots of really small kids sit on the ledge to
throw in bits of bread. I always get nervous watching them.
I just know that one day I'm going to watch some two-
year-old fall into that nasty water. They really need to put
up a rail. I mean, it says a lot if a ten-year-old is worried
about little kids falling, right?

I'm almost there, almost to my bench, when I hear
someone laughing. It sounds real different than anyone
else's laugh. It sounds pretty. I look over and there's this
guy sitting under a tree. He's got his leg bent and his elbow
is on his knee. He's got a book open and he is really
laughing now. I can't tell for sure, but I think maybe even
his eyes are closed, he's laughing so hard. I can't tell what
the book he's reading is. I wish I could. It must be good. I
smile a little and remember to keep walking. I like it when I
see other people who like books a lot like me. It's cool.

There he goes again, laughing real loud. I turn my
head to see and this time he looks right at me. I can't really
see his face too good but he has an awesome smile, it's real
big. I bet the girls in my class would talk about him a lot,
like they talk about Clay Hughes, the cutest boy in the
whole school.

I am finally at the bench. There are a couple of
ducks right in front of me, too. I like that. Mama always
says, "you really like the park, Anna" but not even she
understands how much I love it here. Pretty much nobody
understands me real good. I like watching stuff happen to
strangers. I like being able to hear nothing. I like being able
to not think too much. Most of all, I like the ducks. They
are great when they stick their whole heads under the
water, trying to get a piece of bread. Sometimes one of
them will even fight a little with another, trying to claim a

piece. They swim together, but other than that they pretty much do their own thing. Kind of like my family. We swim together, but that's pretty much about it.

Suddenly, there's the guy next to me. He holds his book and is smiling again.

"Hi there," he says, sitting down next to me.

I just raise my eyebrows and say nothing. It's cool to say nothing.

"I like the ducks. Don't you?"

Mama has told me ten thousand two hundred and forty-three times not to talk to strangers.

So I stay quiet again and just look at the ducks. I'm wondering if maybe he's a weirdo or something and if I should get up and leave. Before I can do that, he holds the book up, waving it.

"This is an awesome book. It's real funny. Even for grown-ups like me."

I don't turn my head all the way, just enough for me to be able to read the title of the book: *The Diary of a Wimpy Kid*. I haven't heard of it.

"It's about this kid who keeps a diary. He's real funny. You wanna look at it for a sec?"

Curiosity got the best of me. I love books. I shrugged one shoulder and took the book. I opened it up and when I read about how the kid said that you had to be careful about which seat you sat down in on the first day of class, lest it become your assigned spot, I couldn't help but laugh a little. I had had teachers who did that: made the first seat you sat down in your seat for the year. When I laughed, I looked back up at the guy, who had sat down next to me. He was looking at the ducks. He was real tanned and he had real dark hair. He was huge, too: way taller than Daddy.

"Pretty funny, huh?" he asked, without looking at me.

"Yeah. I guess."

"You like to read?"

I nod.

"Me too. I like to tell stories, though, even better."

This time, he did look at me. His eyes were so pretty, real blue.

"What kind of stories?"

I couldn't help myself. If he had good stories to tell, I'd be willing to listen.

"Well, all sorts of 'em, really. You wanna hear one?"

I shrugged, looking back at the ducks, trying to look like I didn't care.

"When I was a kid, we used to have this pond that was behind our house. Not right behind it, though. You had to walk along this little pathway through some woods to get to it. The pathway led you through a thicket of hundreds of thousand-year-old trees, trees so tall that they blocked a lot of the sunlight during the day and it was black as night after sunset. One night, long after suppertime, when I should have been in bed, I thought I'd go to the pond. This was a really dumb idea. I could have easily gotten lost and if I'd fallen and gotten hurt, I don't know if I'd ever have been found. But, of course, kids don't think about those things. I just knew I could do it by myself."

"How old were you?"

He lifted a shoulder and tipped his head.

"Don't remember. Just young. Anyway, I snuck out my window and started walking down the path to the pond. Now, over the years, the path had grown worn. It wasn't like I was walking without a trail—there was a faded patch of grass that obviously had been walked on a lot. It was going to be my map. I kept walking, looking down at the trail the whole time. I was kind of nervous and a little bit scared, too. The woods behind our house was home to all sorts of different animals. We'd heard animals that we'd never seen, we thought there might even be a few bears out there somewhere. We knew there were deer—they came right up to our backyard, practically. We knew there were skunks, opossums, rabbits, even some coyotes, those sorts of creatures. I couldn't help but be a little scared, even though I never would have admitted that to anybody. I just knew that there was something different about that night. There was a full moon. It shone bright, real bright. When I looked up, I could barely see its outline through the tops of the trees. It shone kind of blue, like, super bright. Every time I took a step, I could hear the crunch, crunch, crunching of my feet as they stepped on the dry leaves and the twigs. All around me were the sounds of the crickets chirping, and every once in a while I'd hear another animal sound that I didn't recognize that would spook me into walking a little faster. By the time the pond was within my sight, I wouldn't have been surprised to find a real life UFO by the water's edge. My heart was pounding. I was excited, but I was also nervous and scared. I don't know what I thought was going to be at the pond that late at night but what was there was something I could never have imagined."

He paused here and took a deep breath, as if he were thinking about it.

"At first, all I saw was the deer. I saw that he was hurt. He was lying down on his side. I couldn't tell how he was hurt, but it was obvious that he was in pain and that he was hurting. I guess he could have been shot; people did hunt deer in the woods back there, but I didn't see any blood. In fact, I couldn't really see the deer much at all because of the bear."

"The bear?"

"Yeah. The bear. She was massive. Totally brown,

with a huge mangy coat."

"She was attacking the deer?"

The man smiled and shook his head once.

"No. She wasn't attacking the deer. Bears don't usually kill deer, cause deer can outrun them. They're not, you know, friends or anything, though. But this bear was protecting the hurt deer. She nuzzled it with her head, she put her paw on the deer's side, at one point I was even pretty sure I saw her try to lick the deer. I couldn't believe what I was seeing. I hadn't ever heard of a bear protecting anything but its cubs. This one, though, was treating this hurt deer like a cub. I stood behind a tree, and I was real quiet. The bear knew I was there: she kept turning her head to the side, trying to sniff me out. That made me scared because I knew that if she was protecting the deer, I'd be seen as a big threat and she'd probably kill me. After a while, the bear bent its head and started pushing the deer's neck up. She was trying to get the deer to stand up. By this time, I was pretty sure that the deer must have been shot so I didn't think it was going to make it. I knew it couldn't stand up, like the bear wanted it to. But the bear wouldn't give up. She just kept nudging the deer's neck until, finally, the deer moved its leg, as if it were trying to stand. I got so excited when I saw it do that that I jumped a little and made a racket. The bear swung her head around to see what had made the noise, but it was dark and she couldn't see me behind the tree. The deer got spooked, too, and when the bear pushed the deer's neck up again, the deer stood up in a hurry. The deer was clearly disoriented because it tried to turn and it was having a hard time deciding which way to look. The bear start walking, real slow, in front of the deer."

"What did the deer do?"

"Well, it followed the bear, of course. Off they went into the woods. The deer wasn't walking too good—it had

32

hurt its leg. But the bear stayed real close to the deer and I knew that the bear was going to take care of the deer. I was a boy and all, and I was a kid, too, but I almost cried, it was so magical what I saw. I just couldn't believe it. It was a real good thing to see, because it reminded me that sometimes the people we least expect to be our friend or to help us are exactly the ones who will."

I was quiet for a long time. I looked back at the ducks. They were swimming. I liked watching their webbed feet paddle along under the water. I wondered what it would be like to have to swim all the time, to not know what it was like to walk around.

"Was that a true story?"

The man smiled and looked down at me. He lifted a brow and tipped his head.

"All stories are true to the storyteller."

I guessed that was true. It didn't tell me whether the story about the bear was true, but I didn't guess it really mattered. Either way, it was a good story. I hoped I would remember it.

"What's your name?"

"Anna."

"Anna, I'm Ash," he said and held out his hand.

I thought that was funny. Most people didn't try to shake a kid's hand. I put my hand in his, though. When I did, the strangest thing happened: I was suddenly warm all over. His hand was real strong. All of a sudden, I felt safe. I felt like I knew this guy. That was crazy cause I didn't know him. But I felt like I did. It suddenly felt like we were friends and had been for a long time.

"You like stories too, don't you?" he asked.

I nodded.

"Me too. I like 'em a lot. In fact, there's this bookstore I hang out in a lot. I like to read stories there. It's cozy. You'll have to come there sometime. I bet you'd like

33

it. It's called the Book Trunk."

I shrugged.

We sat in silence for a few more minutes before Ash stood. I couldn't keep myself from turning my head to look at him. He smiled.

"I best be going. I'm glad that we got to see each other."

"Yeah."

"See ya."

"Okay."

And away he walked. I watched him walk away and suddenly felt, well, sad. I didn't want him to leave. It was weird but even after just talking for a few minutes, I thought he knew more about me than even my own family did. I didn't know him quite as well. But I wanted to. It made me feel real bad, thinking that I might not ever see this guy again. I watched him walk away for another few seconds. He was really huge—tall as a tree, huge all around. His hands were, like, at least three times bigger than mine. His blue and white plaid shirt and the dark jeans made him look like an advertisement for Stetson. All he needed was the hat. I knew it was dangerous, and all around bad, to talk to adult strangers. But I also *knew* that I was safe with Ash.

I didn't really think much more about it. I just stood up and said, "Ash?"

He turned around and I was so glad that I had called his name. I had never seen anyone look as happy as he did just then. He was really *happy*. His smile was wide and open and his eyes seemed to sparkle.

I shrugged.

"Maybe you could show me how to get to that bookstore you were talking about?"

He winked and then turned, tipping his head. Then

started walking again. I stood, frozen in my spot, until he paused and looked over his shoulder at me.

"Well, are you comin' or not?" he asked.

I felt my face relax into a smile. We walked towards the exit of the park and passed the playground where kids were swinging and sliding and hanging onto the monkey bars. For one of the only times that I could remember, that was really okay with me, cause I had a new friend myself. His name was Ash.

***** ***** *****

Ash sits in front of me, on the floor, his back against the corner of the bookstore wall. He's been in this same position all day. On either side of us are bookshelves that reach all the way up to the ceiling, filled to overflowing with books. The dusty smell of the very small bookstore is the smell of old books, a scent that is sweeter to me than any perfume ever made. The floor is wooden, and it creaks whenever we move. There is only one girl working at the store today, but we haven't seen her since we got here. There are two chairs in the middle of the narrow aisle, but neither me or Ash want one: we like sitting on the floor. Ash says it's better to tell stories when you're comfortable. I haven't known him but for a couple of hours and already I know that Ash should be a writer: he has the best stories ever told, much better than what's in most of the books that now surround us. When I told him that, though, he just smiled.

"I like telling the stories, not writing them."

"Why not?"

He shrugged.

"I'm just not a writer. I do like telling the stories, though."

That's a good thing because I love listening to his

35

stories.

"Do you know another one?" I ask.

He takes a deep breath and reaches out to pat my leg.

"I think the bookstore is going to close soon."

"Just one more?"

He winks.

"Alright. I'll tell you what got me started on lovin' stories so much."

That sounds like it's probably a really good one. I put my hands in my lap and lean back against the bookshelf that's behind me. I'm really comfortable. I could live in this bookstore and be happy the rest of my life.

"Okay, so, when I was a boy, about eight or so, I guess, an old, old, *old* man came to town. He didn't have family there, and he didn't know nobody. He didn't even have a house. He was homeless. But that was kind of the way he wanted it. See, he was what they called a traveling storyteller. He would go from town to town, telling stories to the children. The adults pretended that it was just for the kids but they listened, too. They liked the stories as much as the kids did. Some of the kids were a little scared of him, though. He was homeless, he was old and the only clothes he had were torn and filthy. He never asked for money, although he would accept food if it was offered. And people offered it. Everybody loved him. They didn't treat him like most people treat homeless people today—he was special, and everybody knew it. He didn't tell stories that could have happened in our town; he told stories about magical ships and little kids that had more courage than the bravest soldier. That was the story that made me adore him. It was set way back in the Civil War, back when the South hated the North and all anybody could talk about was what side they were on and Abraham Lincoln. Well, there was a man who wanted to go to war and so he enlisted. He was for the North. He wanted everybody to be treated like people, and he didn't think slavery was a good thing. Besides that, all his family was for the North, too. So off to war he went. The North had the better supplies and the better training, at least most thought so. But this soldier was scared and cold, especially come Christmas when they didn't have the right kind of shoes or enough food to eat. One day, there was a surprise attack on the man's camp. Everybody was shooting rifles and running every which way; his regiment had not been prepared for an attack that morning. The soldier saw a house, and he headed that way, thinking he could find cover behind the house. He was wrong. He might have, if he'd have made it to the house. But he didn't. He was shot before he got there. He was shot bad. He was laying out in the open, bleeding to death. Some of his comrades stopped to see how bad he was hurt, and when they saw they left because they thought he was just about dead. Above him, he could see the smoke from all the rifles firing—and the noise! It was so loud! Rifles firing, people shouting, it was a real mess. The soldier was in a lot of pain and he kept screaming, but he didn't think anyone could hear him. He thought he was about to die. Then he turned his head and there was this little girl. She was younger than you, Anna, and she was barefoot. She had nobody with her. He didn't know where she'd come from, but she was walking towards him—directly into the line of fire! The soldier knew that the girl would get shot. Nobody would intentionally shoot a little girl, but she was in the middle of the fight—it was just going to be inevitable. He screamed at her and told her to turn around, run away, but she didn't. She just smiled at him and kept walking towards him. When she finally got to him, the soldier told her again that she had to leave right then, she had to get cover. Instead, she sat down beside him and touched her finger to his lips, telling him to be quiet. The soldier was so surprised at how unafraid she was, and he was in so much pain, that he did as she wanted him to do and got quiet. The noise was deafening, now, it was so loud. He thought he said as much to the girl. He was worried that her ears would get hurt. Then the little girl moved: she moved to lay down beside the soldier. She wrapped her arms around his waist and she laid down— right beside him, her head on his chest.

Other people were starting to notice the girl. First one soldier stopped firing because he was scared he was going to hit the child. Then another. Then another. Pretty soon, a commanding officer ordered the North to stop firing, then the South stopped, too. The soldiers began inching their way to see what was going on. The girl was still lying with her head on top of the soldier's chest, and then they heard something. It was real soft, she wasn't doing it real loud, so the soldiers, both sides, started walking closer, trying to hear what she was doing. When they got close, they realized she was singing to the wounded soldier. She was singing 'Amazing Grace.' Finally, a medic came up to check on the wounded soldier. The medic looked at the little girl with sad eyes and told her that the soldier was dead. The little girl did something strange then. She smiled. She smiled and she said, 'I know. The noise was bothering him. He's better now.' Then she leaned over and kissed the dead soldier's cheek and stood up. Both armies stood in amazement as they watched her walk away.

The commanding officer of the South tried to find her later. They couldn't. Different soldiers from the North tried to find her, too, to thank her for being there for one of their soldiers at his time of death. They couldn't find her, either. Some said she was an angel. Some said she was the daughter of an officer in the South's regiment. Some wondered if she could have been related to the dead soldier.

No one really knew. Then, some time after the war, citizens of the town where the conflict occurred said that every so often at exactly the same time a little girl with blonde hair could be seen walking hand in hand with a man dressed in a North uniform. It was always at the same time, ten o'clock in the morning. When the citizens did the research and looked up the story, they discovered that that was the exact time that the soldier was pronounced dead by the medic. The town built a monument that stands in that spot today that is dedicated to the 'Brave little hero who offered a soldier compassion at the risk of her own life. Sometimes the greatest gifts of a life come from the smallest of us all.'"

I couldn't speak. All I could do was stare at Ash's face. I didn't even know what to think about the story, except that it was beautiful and I hoped it was true.

"I loved that story so much that later I went to see the monument myself. I made sure to go right at ten o'clock and, sure enough, I saw them. The little girl and the soldier, walking hand in hand. It looked like she was singing to him again and he was listening to her. Sometimes the greatest things are given by the smallest ones."

I smiled a little. I loved that story, too. I didn't know if I really believed him, about his seeing the girl and the soldier, or not, but it was still a beautiful story and I hoped it was true, too. I had heard a lot of beautiful stories today.

"Excuse me."

I heard the voice of the girl who worked in the bookshop.

"I need to close the shop now."

"Oh. Okay. Sorry," I replied and then turned back to Ash.

He was watching me with a smile. Without saying a word, he stood up and then held out his hand for mine. I

39

gave it to him and he pulled me to my feet. I was so glad that we had come to the bookshop. I was so glad that I had made a new friend.

When we got outside, Ash winked at me.

"Better get home," he said.

I nodded.

"Okay."

"You know, you might be a pretty good writer," he said.

"What? Me? No."

"Did you like the stories I told you today?"

My eyes lit up.

"Oh, very much! I loved them!"

"Then you might think about writing them down. That way, you wouldn't forget them."

He had a point. I did not want to forget the stories at all. Not even one sentence of them. Still, I just shrugged and put my hands in my pockets.

"Will I see you again?"

"Maybe, just maybe Ms. Anna."

He winked.

"Ecrivez-moi."

"What's that mean?"

He smiled and turned, headed down the sidewalk in the opposite direction than I needed to go. I watched him leave for a long time before the wind hit me in the face. I needed to get home.

***** ***** *****

All sound is created from vibrations.

That's what I think about when I hear the slap against my cheek. Daddy's hand hit me hard and I could feel the sting in my cheek, kind of like it was vibrating. When his fist came again and hit me in my cheekbone, I heard not only the quiet sound of his hand hitting my skin but it made me fall and I heard the crashing of my hip against the coffee table. I wondered if it was me or the coffee table that vibrated the most, causing the noise. I could hear Daddy telling me that if I ever stayed out that late again, he'd make sure I couldn't walk no more, too, but I couldn't really think about it. All I could think about was the noise. So much noise. My head hurt really bad, I could feel it pounding. It felt like my brain was shaking inside my head. My eyes hurt, too. They were aching.

The next thing I was aware of was that the noise wasn't so loud. Things seemed still. I heard a loud banging and realized that Daddy was gone, he'd went into his and Mama's room. I probably had a couple more hours before she'd come home from work. I had to think of something to tell her about how I got the bruise I was sure was going to be on my face by then. First, though, I needed to get out of the living room. I tried to sit up but the whole room started swimming before me and I couldn't even roll over. Standing up was a dumb idea. My stomach hurt really bad and there was a really awful taste in my mouth. I really wanted to get to my room. I wanted to pull the covers up over my head and not move again. Ever. I've got a blanket on my bed: it's white and has this huge pink heart in the middle of it. It's really, really pretty. Even better, though, it's real warm. It's easy to hide under because it's so thick and heavy. I pictured it in my head and I just wanted to get to it.

Rolling over hurt real bad. It made my head feel like it was a volcano exploding. But then I thought of the little girl in Ash's story, the one who walked out into open fire to lay beside a dying soldier. If she could be brave, then I could be brave, too. I pushed one of my hands up and then the other, until I was on my knees. I still was afraid to stand up because I thought I'd fall back down. I crawled through the hallway to my bedroom. As soon as I stood up to try and climb into my bed, though, I felt sick. I fell onto my bed and closed my eyes. With one hand, I grabbed the cover and pulled it over me. I was warm now. I was safe now. Everything was going to be okay now.

I guess I fell asleep. When I woke up, I felt better. I was really sore, and my body hurt. My face hurt. But my head felt better and my stomach felt better. I wasn't tired anymore, either. I dreamed about seeing a bear help a deer. It seemed like it was so long ago since Ash had told me that story. I sat up in my bed and looked over at my desk. There was a pad of paper on it. Without thinking, I stood up and grabbed it and a pen, then hurried back to the warmth of my blanket.

"THE BEAR'S FRIEND"

That's what I wrote in the notebook, on the first line. Then I started writing down all that I could remember of Ash's story. I tried to keep it exactly like Ash told me. I didn't write down anything but what he'd said in the story. I felt better now. For real. My body still hurt, and I was still afraid that there was more that Daddy would want from me tonight. But I was better. Writing the story, remembering the story, made me smile. I wrote the last line in the story and then I laid the pen down to read it and, as I did, I heard the sound of Ash laughing again. It was such a pretty sound that it made me laugh a little.

All noise is created by vibrations.

I was pretty sure I knew what had vibrated when I laughed that time. It was my heart, waking up.

3
Wishes

My foot keeps thumping against the floor. I try to
pay attention, 'specially now cause Mrs. Keller is giving
our spelling test. I sort of have to pass it cause it gets sent
home in the Weekly Folder, and if my dad sees that I didn't
do good, he wouldn't like it. But it is hard to pay attention.
I have this problem a lot. Mrs. Keller says that my mind
wanders. I don't mean for it to do that, it's just that there's
other stuff going on that seems more important than school.
Especially since getting good grades is hard for me in the
first place. I have to try extra hard, a lot harder than Emily
Grayson, who says she gets paid five whole dollars for
every good report card she brings home. If that's the only
way I could ever get money, I'd never be able to buy
anything, ever.

"Bicycle."

Mrs. Keller has a really soft voice. Sometimes it's
hard for me to hear her, which is another reason I don't
always do so good on these tests. I don't hear her too good
now, either. All I can hear is the thumping of my foot
against the floor. My right thumbnail goes up into the
corner of my mouth. Mama says biting my nails is not a
good habit. Lots of things I do are not good.

"Anna? Do you need me to use the word in a
sentence?"

Mrs. Keller was right in front of my desk. I felt my
face flood with heat again and I jerked my eyes down,
holding my pencil tightly. I nod so that she won't think my
mind was wandering again. Mrs. Keller didn't leave my

desk like I hoped she would. Instead, she stayed there and repeated the spelling word.

"Bicycle. I rode my bicycle to school today."

Bicycle.

B—i—s—e—k—l—e.

I looked at the word and knew it wasn't right. But I didn't know which of the letters were wrong. I'd never have it erased and spelled again before she called out the word for number ten. This test was doomed. I hated this, feeling like all the kids in the class were looking at me. I quickly turned my pencil around and started trying to erase the word I'd just written, the one that wasn't really a real word.

"The last word is 'around.' Around. I turned around to see my pet dog."

I give up.

***** ***** *****

There he is! There he is! He *did* come! He *did!* I am right in the middle of the line of kids trying to get into the cafeteria, but when I stretch my neck up and to the side real hard, I can see him. Ash promised me he would come eat lunch with me, and he did! I can't believe it! Ash is such a great friend. I wonder what story he's going to tell me today. He sits at a long table, kind of by himself. He has a red sweater on that I've always liked, and he is smiling at me. Ash is always smiling. Course, I'm smiling right now, too, cause I always love to see Ash. And it means a lot to me that he came to eat lunch with me. I don't care no more about the stupid spelling test. I will on Friday when Daddy asks me what I think a good 'consequence' would be for another bad grade but, right now, all I care about is that Ash is here. That makes it a good day. Even if I am at school.

"Hey, peanut," he greets me in his really deep, cool voice. He says that God knew He had to give him a great one cause all good storytellers have to have the right kind of voice for their stories. I'm super glad God made him a storyteller, and I'm happy that he gave Ash the kind of voice he's got. It always makes me smile.

"Hi, Ash. Didn't you bring a lunch?" I ask as I sit down to take out my ham sandwich and cup of applesauce.

"You mean you won't share?" he asked, putting a hand over his heart. He likes to pretend a lot. I think that's one of the reasons why we are such great friends. I laugh a little and hand over the cup of applesauce with a spoon.

"So how's your day going?" he asked.

I shrug.

"I had to take a spelling test and I didn't do really good. How do you spell 'bicycle'?"

He tells me. I feel my face squish and I take a bite out of my sandwich.

"Hey, guess what?" Ash asks, putting his elbows on the table and leaning his head down on them to try and look at me. When he does this, a lock of his hair gets in his face. I think that's cute, but I know he doesn't like it cause he shakes his head real fast, making the lock of golden hair swing away again.

"What?"

"I have a really good story. I've been waiting all day to tell it to you. You wanna hear it?"

My smile, with its gap between the front two teeth, is going to break my face. There isn't anything in the world that makes me happier than Ash's stories.

"Now. Tell it to me right now."

Ash smiles, raising his eyebrows playfully, lifting his head.

"Well, once upon a time, in a far, far, far away land there lived a little girl. Her name was Lily. Lily didn't have any brothers or sisters. She didn't have a dad, either. Her mom had to work all the time, so Lily was left by herself in the afternoons after school. She didn't have friends, either."

"Ash, am I going to like this story? You made it seem like it was a great one."

"It is! Just be quiet and listen to it, will ya?"

So I look down and eat another bite out of my sandwich.

"Anyway, she didn't have any friends. But every night she would open up her window and she'd make a wish on a star. She always wished for the same thing. She didn't wish for toys. She didn't wish for clothes. No, instead, she just wished that she could play, just once, just for a little while, with other kids. Well, one day, when she got home from school, she went upstairs into the attic. She was just looking at stuff; she knew her mom had boxes and boxes of things up in the attic, but she didn't know what was in any of them. Most of the boxes just had picture albums and some art things that Lily had made since she was real little. But in one of the boxes, Lily pulled out this old, old leather book. It had a lot of dust on it, and it wasn't really pretty. The pages were yellowed and some of them had a gritty feel to them because it hadn't been looked at in so long. The book didn't have a title on the cover. It was just leather. Lily thought it could have been a journal, maybe that her mom kept a long time ago."

"Mama says it's not nice to read things that aren't yours without askin' first."

"It's a story, Anna. Do you want to know what was in the book, or not?"

I grin.

"Okay. I'll be good now. What was in the book?"

"Well, when –"

"Anna, Anna, she's so dumb she can't even spell bicycle."

I heard a lot of loud laughing behind my back then. But I didn't turn around. I knew who had said it. I knew if I turned around, the laughing wouldn't stop. I felt a hard lump in my throat and tried to swallow past it. I couldn't look at Ash, either, so instead I tried to take a drink of my juice.

"Anna, Anna, dumber than a wheel, she don't know what's real."

"I bet she still believes in Santa Claus."

"And she probably thinks the Tooth Fairy gives her money, too."

They were laughing again.

I slant my eyes upward to see Ash. His deep blue eyes are watching me. He looks sad.

"You should be sitting with a friend."

"I am," I muttered.

"I mean, someone your own age. Would it be better if I came over to your house to tell you my story?"

My head jerks up faster than a bullet and I glare at Ash.

"No!"

I say it so loudly the laughing stops behind my back but all I care about is staring at Ash. He lifts his brows and nods.

"So you do still want to hear the story?"

I nod.

"Good," he says happily. He takes a spoonful of applesauce and eats it. Then he starts telling the story again. I decide I'm going to pretend my classmates are in a different country. Or planet—that would even be better. I want to hear Ash's story.

"Well, when Lily opened the leather book, something magical happened. On the pages were words but, suddenly, the words started coming up off the pages. For real! One letter at a time, they seemed to fly off the

page and dance around Lily's head. Pretty soon, there were
dozens, no hundreds, of letters swirling and twirling
around. Lily's eyes got so big. She couldn't believe what
she was seeing. She tried to read the words, but they were
flying around so fast she couldn't make any of them out.
Then, all at once, the words seemed to change into different
things. Suddenly, right beside her were two little boys.
They had hats on. One of them was laughing. 'Hi!' they
said. 'Would you like to come with us?.' Lily didn't know
what their names were, but she decided that she would go
with them. And so they took her hand and off they ran.
They started running across the attic—except it wasn't an
attic anymore, it was a beautiful savannah and there were
all sorts of wild animals. There were lions over in the
corner behind the stack of three brown boxes. There were
giraffes over by the old air conditioning unit. There was an
elephant, too! It was standing beside her mom's old record
player. Lily was so excited she could hardly stand it. The
second boy then turned and whistled and when he did,
dozens of other children came out from behind the bushes,
from down the trees, from around the tree trunks—there
were children everywhere—many more children than
animals. Suddenly, from out of nowhere, they heard a loud
sound. It was an angry sound, a mean sound. The animals
were spooked: the lion and the cub looked up and darted
behind some trees. The elephants trumpeted. The children
scattered. Even the two boys that had brought Lily here
were scared and ran to hide behind a bush. But not Lily.
She stayed put. She was mad that someone had dared scare
the animals and the other children. The sound came again,
only closer and louder this time. It sounded like something
popping. The sound got louder and louder and louder
until...from behind a huge rock came a boy with a gun.
'Why aren't you running?' the boy asked. Lily put her
hands on her hips. 'You put that gun away right now.' 'Or

what?' the boy asked. 'Or I'm going to pick up these rocks
and throw them at you. I might even erase you out of the
book.' See, Lily knew that this was just part of a story and
she knew that the only way the boy could be real was if he
was part of the story. The boy knew it, too. 'Don't do that!
I'll die if you do that!' 'Then you take that gun and throw it
into the water right this minute.' The boy didn't want to do
it. But the elephants who were watching began realizing
that the boy wanted attention more than he wanted to hurt
anyone. This made the elephants feel confident. They
started acting aggressively, like they were going to charge
him. Finally, the boy gave up. He threw the gun in the
water. Suddenly, the children came out of hiding and so did
the animals. The children were clapping and chanting
Lily's name. They asked Lily if she could teach them a new
game, a game from her country. Lily taught them
hopscotch, and they thought it was very funny. Then they
all played other games, too, some that they taught Lily and
some that Lily taught them. Lily ate the fruit from the trees,
just like the other children did. By the time the sun went
down, Lily's skin was burning: she'd have a terrible
sunburn the next day. But she'd never been happier. She'd
learned a lot of things. She'd learned that sometimes being
brave is just understanding the reasons why someone does
something. She knew now that the kids at school didn't
really hate her, they just didn't want to be ignored
themselves. They just didn't understand Lily. She also
learned that sometimes kids do mean things because they
don't feel good themselves. The boy with the gun
threatened to hurt the animals and children but only
because he had been ignored for so long, and he felt so
alone. And then she learned something else. While they
were playing, Lily looked over and saw the boy who'd had
the gun sitting by himself under a tree. She went over to
him and said, 'Why don't you come play with us? We'd

love to have you play, as long as you're nice to everyone.'
And he did. He did go play with them and Lily learned that,
if she tried hard enough, she could be friends with anyone.
Even someone who threatened to hurt her with a gun.
When finally the boys who had brought her here said she
needed to go home, Lily was happy. Before she went to
sleep, she thanked the stars outside, for she knew that she'd
found the book in the attic and gone on such an adventure
only because the wishing star made her wish come true."

This was a good story, of course. All of Ash's
stories are good ones. But it wasn't as good as some of
them are. He told this story one time about a little girl who
wanted to go to Paris, France, so bad that she stowed away
in an airplane in the cargo bin. That was better. But I still
smiled at him to tell him I'd liked his story and then I
looked back down at my sandwich. Half of it was gone but,
all of a sudden, I just wasn't real hungry anymore. My
stomach felt kind of queasy, too.

"Anna? What? You didn't like the story?"
I shook my head.
"No, no, I did. I did like it. Really."
He frowned, tipping his head to the side.
"Then what's wrong? Those kids got you upset?"
I shook my head no, although that was a lie.
"I just—I know it was just a story and all but..."
"But what?"
The bell rang. Lunch was over. I tossed my half-
eaten sandwich into the bag and stood. I reached over to
take his cup of applesauce and the spoon. Throwing it all
into the nearest trash can, I shrugged my shoulders.
"Wishes don't really come true."
Ash opened his mouth to say something, but then
closed it again. Finally, he winked.
"Ecrivez-moi, Anna."

My cue to go. I smile at him again and wave. It's time to go back to class.

Ash never lies to me. Ever. Not even those little lies that Mama says some people tell so that they don't hurt your feelings. Ash never lies. And that's why he didn't try to tell me that wishes can come true.

***** ***** *****

There are lots of wishes I'd like to see come true. Like, I wish I was friends with Emily Grayson so that she could teach me how to make good grades. There's this girl in my class named Amanda and she has a pair of awesome sneakers: they are tie dye with colorful rhinestones all over them. The coolest part is that when she walks, the shoes light up. I wish they were my sneakers. I wish my hair was black. I wish my mom and dad would never fight. But, I'd give up those wishes, and would never ask for another wish as long as I live, if I could somehow make God or a wishing star make Daddy stop coming to my room. That's what I really wish for.

I think about Ash's story. Lily was brave. Ash wanted me to be brave, too. That's why he told me the story, I know it was. But I'm not Lily. I'm not brave. I'm pretty dumb, like the kids at school say I am. I mean, I couldn't even spell bicycle. And my mind wanders a lot, too. Special kids, good kids, are the ones who are brave. But I can't stop thinking about the story. I liked how all the other kids, the ones that Lily thought were cool, ran and hid at the first sound of danger. Lily was a good kid. I bet the animals loved her after that. I hope I don't forget the story. That thought makes me so sad that I throw the covers off me. I know I'm not supposed to turn on my bedroom light; if I do, I could get in trouble. So I just grab my story notebook and open it to a blank piece of paper. I like seeing

51

the blue lines against the white backdrop. I like rubbing my hand across the paper. I really like writing all of Ash's stories down. He says that makes us a great team: he likes to tell them, and I like to write them. I like seeing the words I wrote cover the lines. It makes me feel safe when I write. I don't feel so dumb when I am writing, not even when I finish writing the story and go back and read it. One time, I read the story back to Ash, to make sure I'd gotten it all right. He said I did a good job of writing down the story he'd told me. He said I have talent. I wish he was right.

I roll my head to the side and stare out my window. It is always so quiet at night. The stars are out. Some of them are so small. Some of them are bigger. Mama says that it's impossible to count all of the stars. She says that's a good thing, though, cause it means that there's enough stars for all the wishes that I could ever want to make. I wonder if it matters if I make the wish on a big star or if it would still come true if I sent the wish to a smaller star? I choose one, it's a big one, and I make my wish. I don't think it'll come true. But I don't guess it can hurt, either. And you never know. Maybe it will come true.

I am thinking of Ash when I close my eyes. I hope he comes to see me tomorrow. Maybe he'll tell me a new story. Or maybe he'll just play with me. Maybe I can read him the story about Lily. Or maybe one day I'll have to come up with a story to tell Ash. That would be neat. I bet he would like that. Except I probably couldn't do it right. I am really sleepy right now, and I can't help but close my eyes.

***** ***** *****

There is heavy breathing tickling the hairs on my neck. Hot puffs of air blow onto my face. My body hurts and it is hard to breathe. My eyes pop open but I do not scream. I feel hands on the top of my hair, pushing my head down. I squeeze my eyes shut, trying to block out everything I see. When the hard thing is pushed into my mouth, I gag and tears appear out of nowhere in the backs of my eyes. My own breathing becomes shallow and quick. It is really hard to think right now. All I want to do is crawl away somewhere, clamp my mouth shut and disappear. I have to remind myself not to bite down. I don't want to hurt my dad. I just feel a need to lock my mouth. But I can't cause the hard thing is in and then out, in, then out. I am sure I am going to be sick. I feel myself gag again and, finally, he stops. The hard thing is gone, but I have made him mad because I gagged. He says good girls don't do that. That is why he pulls me up by my hair again. I can't stop the short scream that rips from my throat when the sticking part happens. The ceiling above my head is moving back and forth, as my body is pushed up then down; I try to keep my eyes on the crack above my head, but it is hard to do.

I don't know how long it lasts. I never do. But finally it is over. He tells me that he loves me and that I can go back to sleep now. Then he's gone, and I hear the door click behind him. He won't be back tonight. I am shaking everywhere. I am sore everywhere. What hurts the most, though, is how I can't hardly breathe. I am really hot, too. I lay still, except for the shaking, which is getting worse, especially in my legs, and stare at the ceiling. Suddenly, I can't see cause the tears are blurring everything. I don't even know why I'm crying. I close my eyes and a tear rolls down the side of my nose. My tongue darts out to grab it and I realize my mouth hurts, too. I really need a drink of water, but I can't move. There is a roaring inside my head, and it is shaking so much I think my brain is going to pop. I turn my head to stare out the window.

There are lots of stars, still. I look up again, at my ceiling. Ash's story was make-believe. It wasn't real. And it's dumb to make wishes when you know they don't come true.

4
If Only

Emily Grayson has glasses now.

She didn't used to have glasses. She just got them. She kept asking to sit in the front of the classroom, and our teacher thought it was cause she couldn't see the board. Everybody's been talking about how cool her glasses are. A couple of kids have called her "four-eyes" but not very many. Nobody ever really talks about Emily cause she's really great. She always has the coolest stuff—like her tie-dye sneakers that I really want. The glasses are almost neater than the sneakers. They are gold along the edges and they are super-thin—you can't hardly tell that she has them on at all, especially with her hair. She's got really, really long black hair that falls to her waist. I've always wanted my hair to be black. You'd think that the black hair would make the glasses stand out more, but it don't.

Emily Grayson is one of those kids that everybody knows just has it all together. She's a good student; the teacher is always calling on her to answer stuff. She volunteers to answer the questions, too. When I'm called on to answer a question, I get really hot and really embarrassed. And I'd rather pee my pants than volunteer to stand up in front of everybody to answer a question. When Emily Grayson does it, though, it seems like the thing to do.

Of course, she's got lots of friends. I used to think that this was cause she was nice to everybody. One time, when we went on a field trip to the pumpkin patch, Emily saw that I was eating by myself at the teacher's table and she asked me to come sit by her. It almost made me cry, that was so nice. I mean, she's not my friend or anything.

55

She doesn't talk to me most of the time and when she gets to choose teams, she never chooses me to be on her team. But that's just because I'm…well…*me* and she's *Emily*.

Mama says that God tells us in the Bible we're not supposed to covet stuff. I didn't know what that meant until she explained it to me. She said one time her best friend got a really pretty dress to wear to her school dance. She said it was gold and had ruffles at the bottom. She said it looked like something Cinderella might wear. Mama wanted that dress real bad. She said that's what coveting means—when you want something that somebody else has real bad. I don't covet most anything. I don't really even care about the kids' cool clothes or their iPods or their Nintendo DS video games. Whenever I hear one of them say that they got something new like that, I just remind myself that I can have whatever I want by making up a story about it. And I do. And it always makes me feel better. Well, almost always.

See, I *covet* Emily Grayson's glasses. When I see her with them on, I think she's smart. I hate school cause I'm not smart. I could wear my hair like she does, too, so I'd be prettier. Maybe if I had glasses, people would want to talk to me. They might think I was smart, too.

The bell rings.

It's time to go home.

***** ***** *****

I like the sound of the water rushing in the bathtub. I pretend it's a waterfall. Mama showed me not too long ago how to take a shower instead of a bath. It was neat when she showed me how I could stand under the water the whole time, instead of sitting in it. I always make her think that I like showers best cause it's more grown-up. At the start of the year, there was this girl named Amanda that was in my class. She was kind of my friend—she talked to me and stuff. We liked to hang out at recess. One day, she told me that her mom showed her how to shave her legs. I thought that was neat cause Mama just started letting me shave my legs this year, too, when I asked her how old I had to be before I could.

Amanda said, "Do you bend your legs when you shave your knees or do you keep your legs straight?"

I didn't know the right answer. Most of the time, I bend my legs. It's hard, and sometimes I get cut a little but I thought that was the way everybody did it.

I didn't want to sound dumb, though, so I just said, "Oh, it's always different. How do you do yours most of the time?"

"I always keep my legs straight, of course. That makes it a lot easier."

"Yeah, that's the way I do it most of the time, too."

That was a lie, but it was a lie that made me feel like I was a little smarter than I really was.

I bet Amanda likes showers the best.

It's the grown-up, cool thing.

But I don't. I don't like feeling the water running over me. It makes me nervous. Baths make me feel a lot better. And, like I said, I love the sound of the water rushing from the faucet. Sometimes I lean back against the tub and stick my toes in the water. I pretend that I'm a dolphin and I'm rushing through the waves of the ocean, trying to help somebody who's fallen off a boat. I should write that story down. It would probably be a good one. Maybe I'll ask Ash if he knows a story about a dolphin. When I'm done with my story, I look at my fingers in the water. I think it's neat how they get all wrinkled when I stay in the water a long time. It makes me wonder what would happen if I stayed in the tub all night—would I just shrivel up all the way? One day, I might try it.

But not today.

I've been in the water so long that it's starting to get a little cold. I don't like anything cold. Cold air reminds me of bad things, like the rush of air I feel right after Daddy gets up off me. I like the warmer water much better. Besides, Mama always takes a bath before she goes to work, so I have to get out pretty soon anyway. When I do, I grab the blue terry towel that is my favorite and wrap it around me. When I pretend that I'm a grown-up, I throw my head over and wrap the towel around my wet hair. I know how to twist it and tuck the end of the towel under in the back to make it look like Mama.

I don't do that today, though.

Instead, I stand in front of the mirror and look at my face.

On my neck, I have a half moon of freckles that I have never liked. My skin looks really pale, like Casper the ghost's. Except my nose. Right now, my nose is really pink. I don't know why. There's a patch of red, too, on my forehead, above the bush that is my right eyebrow. My eyes are okay. They are really blue. Everybody says that's a good thing. I guess so. They are really small, though. I touch the thumb of both of my hands to my first fingers. It makes a circle. Then I hold the circles up over my eyes and look into the mirror, trying to see what I might look like with glasses. I think I'd look pretty with them. Especially the kind that Emily Grayson's got. I lean my face in towards the mirror a little more, trying to see better. I bet if Mama took me to an eye doctor, he'd say I really do need glasses. I have to hold the books up a lot closer to my face than some of the other kids in my class, who can read a book that's lying on their desk.

"Anna? Are you almost done in there?"

I hear my mom's voice standing outside the bathroom and jerk into action, lowering my hands again and finally rubbing my body dry. It makes me want to have clothes on right away. I don't like being naked. I forget about my face and my eyes and glasses and hurry to get dressed.

"I'm almost done," I call back, before she can come in to check on me.

I don't like anyone seeing me naked, not even my mom.

***** ***** *****

I sit with my feet curled up to my chest, next to my bedroom door. I want to be in my bed. But I don't want to move. Moving is scary. So I will stay here instead. I don't know how long I've been here. I woke up a little while ago cause I heard my dad yelling. I wake up a lot to listen to their fights. They are always about the same thing: some apartments that we used to live in when I was a baby. I don't remember living there, but I don't like it whenever we have to drive by there now. I've heard this fight so many times that I sort of know what happened, but not really. All I know is that Mama gets really mad cause Daddy saw some lady named Kate. I mean, really mad. That's okay, cause Daddy gets really mad, too. I don't know which of them gets more mad. But whenever this fight starts, it goes on most of the night. I almost always wake up and get real scared cause sometimes they start doing more than yelling. I've seen my mom get knocked down. I've seen my mom hit my dad. I've seen lots of bad stuff. It's scary when you think that your mom or dad might get hurt.

Here's what will happen.

Sooner or later, my dad will walk out of the house. He don't go nowhere, but it's his way of telling Mama that he's done. One time, he got in the car and did actually leave, I think cause he was scared Mama wasn't going to stop until he was out of her sight. But he called a little bit later and was home before I was supposed to have ever known he left in the first place. Anyway, after he leaves, Mama comes into my room. I will pretend to be asleep, cause I don't want her to know that I'm scared, and cause I know I probably ain't supposed to listen to the fights. She'll lean down and kiss me on the forehead and hug me. Her skin is always cold and sweaty then. She'll whisper she's sorry and then she'll leave the room. A lot of the times, she is crying. Then she'll leave. The house will get real quiet and I'll be able to fall asleep again. When I wake up, everything is back to normal. Mama will help me get ready for school, feed me breakfast, and make sure I catch the bus. Daddy will be getting ready for work and he'll tell me good morning, too. He might give me a hug and tell me to have a good day. Mama and Daddy won't talk to each other at all. I'll go to school and come home, eat dinner, take a bath and go to bed. Then Mama will go to work, and Daddy will come in my room.

I guess since I've seen it so many times and I know what's going to happen, it shouldn't scare me like it does, but I can't help it. I shake a lot. And I cry, too. I can feel my teeth start to grind.

Suddenly, the door to my room cracks open a bit and in walks the new puppy. Mama says that when he gets bigger, he might have to stay outside. For now, though, he can sleep inside. I am happy about that. He is real cute. He's very playful. He climbs up in my lap and licks my face. I pet him, but then I hear Mama call Daddy a bad word. Daddy gave the dog to me. Daddy hurts me. Daddy hurt Mama, too. I put the dog back on the floor and shoo him away, then I scramble up to my bed before he can come back and get in my lap again. I know I'm a bad girl but I wish Daddy wasn't even here at all.

The house is real quiet.

I don't hear nothin' at all.

I look towards my window. I can see the sun coming in. In the mornings, when I wake up, it always looks kind of grayish blue, instead of real bright. There's a lot of fog, too. It makes it hard to see. I like that 'cept that the fog also makes it colder. I probably won't be able to walk to school today. I will probably have to ride the bus. Mama don't like me walking if it's foggy or cold or rainy. She says it's dangerous. Last night, after Mama came in to tell me she was sorry, I put on the clothes I wanted to wear to school today. I do that a lot. I will go to sleep in my pajamas but wake up in the middle of the night and change into my school clothes. See, I don't like being naked, 'specially when it's real bright. I don't really even like changing clothes in my bedroom. I used to get, like, real shaky and scared and stuff whenever I had to take a bath. If I do it real fast in the middle of the night when I know everybody else is asleep and it's dark in my room, changing clothes is a little bit easier. Plus, it means I don't have to rush around in the morning. Mama says I get ready fast. She don't know that I change into my daytime clothes in the middle of the night.

By the time I walk out of my room, I hear Daddy in their room down the hall. I turn my head and see him opening the sock drawer. He looks towards me and smiles.

"Morning, peaches."

"Good morning," I mumble.

"Your mama's downstairs making pancakes. I'll be down soon."

I nod and keep walking.

Maybe I can be on the bus before he gets downstairs to eat breakfast.

Our house is super cold. Our stairs are wooden and they are always cold. I wish I hadn't forgotten to put my socks on before I left my bedroom. But, I did. I'll have to wear the ones from yesterday that are still stuck inside my shoes by the front door. When I get to the kitchen, Mama is pouring orange juice into my favorite blue cup, the one that nobody ever uses but me.

"Hey there," she says, smiling at me.

Mama is pretty. Everybody says so. She's got real pretty hair that comes to her waist, and her skin is tanned. She says that one time there was this guy who came up to her at the park and told her he wanted to take pictures of her. She laughed and rolled her eyes when she told me about it, but I could tell that it had made her happy that the guy told her that. I guess girls like to be pretty. Normal girls anyway.

I grab a plate and sit down to eat.

"Do you have anything due at school today?" Mama asks, sitting down across from me.

Her eyes are red and puffy. She don't think I do, but I know it's cause she's been crying a lot. That's what happens to my eyes when I cry myself to sleep, too.

I shake my head.

"No."

"No tests?"

"Not til Friday."

"That's good."

I nod.

"Who did you say has new glasses?"

"Emily Grayson."

"That's right. The nice girl."

I nod again, looking down at my pancakes.

"Maybe you can ask her to play hopscotch with you or something at recess."

Nobody ever plays hopscotch anymore. But I don't tell Mama that. I just nod. Again.

"I hope no one teases her because of her new glasses," Mama says. "Glasses make you smart, because you can see better with them, so it's easier to learn stuff."

"I guess so. She has lots of friends."

"That's good."

I keep eating my pancakes.

"Do you want a banana?" Mama asks.

Mama has to talk a lot when she's trying not to cry. I know that about her. I shake my head and keep my eyes on my pancakes. I am taking really big bites now. I am almost done with them. I sneak a glance at the clock above the sink. The bus won't be here for another fifteen minutes. By then, Daddy will be downstairs. By then, I could be almost to school.

"Can I walk to school today?"

Mama frowns and looks out the window at the fog. I can tell she is about to say no.

"Please. It's just up the road. I know the way and I walk home even when it's not real bright outside sometimes. I'm not a little kid."

Mama sighed and put her fork down, her eyes growing serious.

"Okay. But you take my cell phone and call the house when you get there."

"I could get in trouble for having a cell phone at school. Please, Mama."

She looked again out the window, thinking about whether or not the fog was enough to tell me no.

"I don't know, Anna. I really don't like you walking at all, especially when you can't see too good."

"I see fine."

63

She smiled.

"Alright, alright. Just be careful, okay."

I feel myself smile and push back my chair in my hurry to get up. I walk over to her and give her a big hug around the neck.

"Thanks!"

"Aren't you going to finish your breakfast?"

"I'm done," I say, reaching over to the counter and grabbing my book bag.

My shoes are by the front door. I'll have to put them on in a minute.

"Be careful, Anna."

"I will!"

***** ***** *****

I was two houses past mine when I felt somebody coming up behind me. I turned around and there was Ash. He grinned.

"Perfect timing, peanut. I came to see if I could walk you to school today."

I smile broadly.

"You did?"

"Yup."

"That's great. Mama almost didn't let me walk at all. She don't like it when I walk, when it's foggy outside."

"That's probably a good Mama."

I nod and shift my book bag higher up on my shoulder. Ash snaps a finger and holds out his hand.

"Give it to me."

"What?"

"The bag, silly."

I smile and shake my head.

"I can carry it."

He shrugs and takes his hand away.

"Do you have a story to tell me?" I ask.

"Actually, I thought you would have a story to tell me."

"I can't tell stories."

"Of course you can. Anybody can tell a story. It's not a matter of being able to tell a story or not. It's a matter of whether or not you're gonna let the story inside you come out."

I don't say anything for a few minutes. The fog does make it a little cooler out than normal. I look up at Ash. He is wearing a black sweater that makes him look even more cute than usual. His dark eyes are smiling. He is wearing a black ski hat today, too, which I think looks funny. I tell him that, too. His face scowls up in mock horror and he puts a hand on the top of his head.

"What? You don't like my hat?"

I laugh.

"It makes you look silly."

"Yeah?"

"Yeah."

"Well, Ms. Fashion Know-it-All, *I* happen to *like* my hat. I think it makes me look cool."

I laugh a little again and shake my head.

"You know what?"

"What?" he asks, as he skips two steps ahead of me. I think he is funny, always acting and trying to play all the time.

"My teacher gave us this homework project. We have to write a short story about a tree."

"A tree, huh?"

"Yeah."

"Have you started it?"

"No."

I see a crack coming up in the sidewalk and step over it carefully with my left foot.

"But I have an idea for it. It's kind of dumb, though."

"You won't know that until you write it and give it to your teacher."

I don't say anything.

"What about if you write it and I read it *first*? If I think something needs to be done to it to make it perfect, you know I'll tell you. I mean, it's a story, right?"

I nod.

"Well, there you go. I might love ya, kid, but a story is a story. It's gotta be right. So, how 'bout it? You get to writing that story about a tree, and then you let me read it."

"You'll tell me the truth about it?"

"Of course."

"Okay."

"Good! I will get to hear a story you wrote after all."

Ash is good at making me smile.

***** ***** *****

The teacher lays the paper, face down, on my desk in front of me. She then goes to the next kid and gives her a piece of paper. I feel really nervous as I lift up the edge of the paper she laid down in front of me and turn over just a little piece of it. *F.* My face is hot and I just about feel like I have to cry. I just *can't* pass a math test. I *can't.* My brain just don't work right, and no amount of studying will fix it. It's, like, broken. An *F* on a test means that either Mama or Daddy has to sign it and I have to give it back to the teacher by Friday. If I don't, she calls them to tell them about it. If I do, Daddy will hurt me.

The tears are almost real now.

I cross my arms over my desk and bury my head in them.

"Okay, class, it's about time for recess. Please put your books away, except your Social Studies workbook. We'll start with that after recess."

Kids start putting things away but I am afraid that if I have to see that big red *F* on my paper right now again, I will start to cry. That would be very embarrassing. So I leave my head on my arms for another minute. I feel like a tree stump. When I finally lift my head and start putting things away, my fingers feel clumsy. I knock one of my notebooks off onto the floor by accident and somebody laughs about it. I feel like they are all talking about me. I feel like everyone is looking at me. When I bend down to get the notebook, I feel fat. I feel ugly. I *am* ugly. And dumb, too. This makes, like, the tenth test I have failed all year in math. I don't know how I am ever going to pass.

"Row one, please go ahead and line up now. Quietly."

The kids in the row ahead of me get up. I hear one of them ask Emily, "What did you get on the test?" and Emily's response: "An A. What did you get?"

By that time, they are already far enough away from me that I can't hear the boy's answer. Of course Emily got an A. She's smart, she's pretty and she's got glasses. That's when I look at Emily's desk and see that her glasses are laying on her desk. She can't wear them to recess. I guess cause she don't need to read outside.

"Row two, please line up."

I stand up and walk to get in line. I don't like standing in line. People are too close to me. I just keep my eyes on the teacher and wait for us to start moving. Finally, we're led outside where we are told to sit in a group. Recess is another word for gym. Before we can have real free time, we have to play some group games. I hate this. First of all, I'm terrible at sports. Second of all, I always feel like I'm waiting in line to die during the group process.

Only the most athletic kids are chosen to pick teams. Since I am not athletic, that is never me. Since nobody knows who I am, nobody ever picks me to be on their team. I'm, like, the leftover player. Finally, the teacher tells us to stand up. We are going to play volleyball. By the time the choices are made, I'm the one who's standing tall, trying to show this is dumb and I don't even care that I'm the last one standing. I'm assigned to the team who is short one player and we all get into our places across the net.

I do try.

I know how to play volleyball. I mean, I know the rules. I'm just not very good at it. But I do try. When I see the ball coming toward me, I try to knock it back over the net. I am close to the net, so this shouldn't be hard. But I totally miss the ball and land up falling on my face.

"Oh man," I hear the other kids on my "team" say.

"You're supposed to HIT the ball," says another one.

I am done. I am so, so done.

I walk off the court and go up to my teacher. I ask if I can go inside to go to the bathroom. She tells me I can.

I walk into the school. Its halls are so bright. The walls are white, but there are art projects displayed on two bulletin boards. I wonder if all schools are so bright. The bathroom is close to my room. I go in and use the bathroom, trying to take as much time as possible. I think I will go into the classroom and get my story notebook. I can write the story about the tree while the other kids are playing. That way, I might have it ready to show Ash by this afternoon.

I walk into my classroom and up to my desk. The story notebook is in my book bag. I get it and start to turn around when something catches my eye on the desk in front of mine. It is Emily's glasses. Emily was the first one chosen for the teams outside. She made an A on the math test that I made an F on. I really wanted those glasses.

I just reached out and took them and stuck them in my book bag. It was real easy, but I got really nervous. What if someone saw me? What if I got caught? I almost put them back but I didn't. Instead, I turned and walked out of the classroom. I forgot to bring my story notebook with me, though. That was okay. I wouldn't have been able to write a story anyway. All I could think about were the glasses in my book bag. Maybe they would make me smart.

***** ***** *****

Everyone looked for the glasses.

Emily noticed they were gone right away, of course, and told the teacher. The teacher thought she might have taken them outside, but Emily promised she hadn't. Then the teacher thought she might have left them in music class or maybe art class. Emily promised they were on her desk when everyone went outside. The teacher made all the other kids look for her glasses. I started to feel a little bad when Emily started to cry. But I still didn't tell the teacher I knew where the glasses were. I pretended to look for them. At the end of the day, the principal came on the intercom to give the afternoon announcements and he even mentioned them. He asked that if anyone found them, please return them to the office. He said that they were important. I did not know that it would be such a big deal.

I hoped Ash would come by today so that I could show them to him.

I would wear them while I did my homework and maybe I would get the answers right this time.

I was excited about the glasses when I got home.

I went into my room and took them out of my book bag. They were really pretty. They weren't heavy at all —

they were really light. They needed to be cleaned, though; there was dust on them from when they were in my book bag. I didn't know what to clean them with. I went into the bathroom and ran water over them and then I took some toilet paper and dried them off. It seemed to work okay. I put them on. Suddenly, the world went fuzzy. I couldn't see anything at all, and my head started hurting almost right away. I took the glasses off again. The world was clearer. Wow. Emily could *see* with these things on? That was really amazing. I put them on and tried to look at myself in the mirror. But I couldn't see anything—all I could see were lines. Everything was way too close. And the headache! I took the glasses off again and looked at them. These things were really strong. I knew that Emily used them to read. Maybe that was the trick.

I took them back into my room and got out my story notebook. I put the notebook in front of me, open, and then I put the glasses on. The words seemed really weird—they were thick and fat, and really blurry. I squinted, but that didn't help. I took them off again. These were useless. They were pretty, but I couldn't even wear them.

For the first time, I started thinking about Emily. These glasses were very strong, almost magic like, especially if they really helped her see stuff. Emily was nice to me. She wanted me to sit with her at lunch that one time. She hadn't done anything mean to me.

"Anna?"

Quickly, I stuffed the glasses back in my book bag, right before Mama opened the door.

"Hey there."

"Hi."

Mama came in and smiled at me. She saw my story notebook. I remembered it was open and I shut it before turning to sit facing her.

"Hey, I thought me and you could have a movie night. I've got popcorn popping. We could watch *Homeward Bound*. What do you say?"

"Okay, sure."

"Great. Come on, then. I want to hear about your day at school."

***** ***** *****

The dogs in *Homeward Bound* are so good, 'specially Chance. I like Shadow, though, too. He's a lot like Ash. Mama reaches over and grabs a handful of popcorn from the big bowl that sits between us. We do this sometimes. Have a movie date, just me and Mama. I like it.

"So, your teacher called," Mama said, suddenly, just as the movie was about over.

"She did?" I ask, turning my head to look at her.

"Yeah. She said that she was calling all the kids' parents. Apparently, Emily lost her glasses today."

I nod.

"Yeah. We had to look for them and everything."

"But you didn't find them?"

I shake my head.

"No."

Mama nods. Then she looks back at the movie.

"Well, that's sad. Glasses are really important. Emily can't see really well without them."

"I know. That's what the principal said, too."

"Maybe she'll find them."

I nod again and, suddenly, I don't feel so good. I don't like lying. I don't like knowing where the glasses are. But if I tell what I did, I'd get in lots of trouble. Trouble at home *and* trouble at school. Being in trouble scares me really bad. So I don't say anything. But I keep thinking about it. It was something how nobody thought of me. It was crazy how nobody thought to look in my book bag. I mean, I'm the worst kid in class. If I were the teacher, I'd have thought to look in the worst kid in class's book bag for something that came up missing. I didn't mean to hurt Emily. I just wanted to be smart, like her. But the stupid glasses don't even work right. At least not for me.

The rest of the night passes. Daddy doesn't come to my room. But I dream about glasses. I am very lucky that I didn't get in trouble for taking the glasses. I know I shouldn't have done it. When I wake up the next morning, the puppy is laying on the bed beside my face. I see him and reach out to pet his head.

"Your name is Lucky."

By the time I get to school, I am nervous again. I know what I have to do. But I don't know how to do it. I got to school really early. I hope that helps. It does. When I walk into my classroom, no one is there. Not even the teacher. Before I can chicken out, I take the glasses out of my book bag and I put them on Emily's desk. Then I leave the room and go into the bathroom. I will just hide so that no one will know I was the one who put the glasses back on Emily's desk, right where I took them from. I walk into a stall and I sit there, behind a closed stall door, until I hear the morning announcements start. Then, as calmly as I can, I walk out of the bathroom and back into my class. I pretend I am just getting to school.

Emily Grayson is smiling and wearing her glasses.

5
The Pretzel Airplane Bird

Ash stood next to me. Both of us had our arms behind our backs and we were leaned forward, trying to see all the different flavors of ice cream behind the glass. I like to copy Ash. When he does something cool, which is almost all the time, I try doing it, too. It makes me feel like I'm almost as neat as he is. Right now, we're trying to decide which type of ice cream to buy.

Today is a good day. For one thing, it's Saturday, which means I don't have to go to school and I get to spend more time with Ash. For another thing, Daddy went to see my grandparents in another city and won't be home tonight. This means I *know* Daddy won't come to my room tonight. This makes me feel...lighter, happier, freer. And *thirdly*, just before I came to the park, where I kind of thought Ash might be waiting for me, I checked my piggybank. It's where I save all the loose change that I find lying around the house. In it, I had nine dollars and sixty-three cents. This means that I have enough money to buy not only myself an ice cream but Ash an ice cream, as well. I feel grown-up. I feel special. I feel important, being able to buy him a special treat. Today will be a good day.

"What kind do you like to get?" I asked, tipping my head towards him.

The girl behind the counter looked my way but when she saw that I was talking to someone else, looked away again. Ash frowned and shook his head. Then he stood up straight again.

"How many different flavors are there?"

73

"They say on TV that they have thirty-two."

"I think I'd like to taste test all thirty-two before I decide."

A grin is tugging at his mouth. He arches his eyebrows and nods.

"I'd like to start by tasting lime," he says.

"Uh—"

"Do they allow taste tests here?"

I smiled.

"I don't know."

"Why don't we ask and find out?"

I shrugged. I looked up towards the girl.

"Excuse me."

She comes over.

"Could I taste the lime? I've never had it before."

"Sure."

She grabs a white spoon and dips some lime on it. Then she hands it to me. I turn and hand it to Ash. He licks a little bit of it off and then hands it back down to me. I try it, too.

"Hm. What about raspberry?" Ash asked.

I ask the lady for a taste of raspberry, and Ash and I repeat the taste test. I am ready now to choose my flavor but Ash decides he needs to try a bite of the lemon. I don't really want to ask the lady for a third taste test. I know we're not supposed to do that. But Ash smiles at me. He has the prettiest smile. I ask for the lemon. The lady sighs heavily and gets me a taste. While she prepares it, Ash uses his elbow to poke me in the side. I look up at him and he makes a silly, angry face. He is laughing because the lady is getting irritated. I frown and shake my head. Anger is not funny. She hands us the lemon. Then I get ready to order the kind I want.

"I think I need at least one more taste test," Ash said.

I look up at him.

"Ash…"

"Come on, one more. I'm not sure yet. I really need to taste the sherbet."

I quietly ask for another taste test with the sherbet. The lady scowls at me but gets it ready.

I am poked again by Ash. When I look at him, he sticks out his tongue and puts his hands on his hips, then looks at the lady. I can't help but laugh cause he is so silly. And it is kind of funny, asking for taste tests, even though we don't need to. After this taste test, Ash tells me he wants the sherbet. I order a double dip sugar cone sherbet.

Once she had it ready, I said, "I want to order one more, but can I try the butter pecan first?"

Ash's shout of laughter is my reward. He takes his sherbet from me and winks.

"Atta girl," he said.

The lady is frowning at me, but I don't care. I am smiling so big now my face hurts. Ash is happy.

***** ***** *****

"You have a chocolate face," Ash tells me a little bit later.

We took our ice cream out of the store because we made the lady mad. We are sitting by the ducks in the park, the same place we first met. I really like this park. I take my hand and wipe away my chocolate face.

"I didn't really need the taste tests, you know. I always get chocolate," I said.

Ash smiles and looks toward the ducks.

Then he leaned sideways, closer to me, and said in a loud whisper, "I always get sherbet."

I laugh at the look on his face.

"Sometimes it's fun just to have fun," said Ash.

I think about that for a minute before I shrug.

"I don't like it when people get mad at me."

"I know."

He takes a bite out of his ice cream and then shrugs.

"But anger isn't a bad thing, not by itself it's not. I get mad a lot," Ash said.

"You do?"

"Oh sure."

"Why do you get mad?"

"Well, for lots of reasons. If I can't remember a story the way I want to, I get mad. Sometimes I even get mad if I can't go to sleep at night, or if I wake up and can't go back to sleep."

He shakes his head.

"But, when I get mad, I tell myself a story, or sometimes I just go somewhere by myself. That makes it better."

I nod.

"Do you ever get angry, Anna?"

I think about this for a minute. Then I shake my head.

"No."

"Never?"

"No."

"What about at the kids at school? When they laugh because of something you do?"

"No. I feel embarrassed but that's not the same thing as being mad."

"You're right, it's not. What about when you think you should be able to do something, like maybe pass a test, but you can't do it?"

I shake my head.

"Nope. I just cry then."

"Hm."

He takes another bite of his ice cream. His is gone now. I still have a little of mine left. Ash tips his head back to look at the sky. It is a really pretty day today. The sky is so bright and blue, and it's not at all cold. It's not hot, though, either. It's really perfect. I wish it could stay like this forever.

"Guess what?" I asked all of a sudden.

I take the last bite of my ice cream and then wipe my hands on my jeans.

"What?"

"I finished my story about the tree. You know, the one we had to do for school?"

"You did? Hey, I want to hear it. How about we go over yonder, in a shady spot, so you can tell it to me?"

"Okay."

We get up and start walking. Everything is so pretty at the park. I like all the flowers. Whenever I see the gardens, with their hedges and decorations, I always wonder who came up with the idea for it to look this way. The gardens at the other park, the one Mama likes, don't look like these. These are bigger. It must have been really hard, making just green grass look so neat and pretty. The tree that we are walking toward is in the center of the biggest garden. That's cause this tree is the biggest one in the park—it stands by itself. Around it are smaller gardens of different types of flowers. It is one of my favorite places in the park.

Ash stretches out on the ground. His red shirt has ridges down the front of it. It makes him look really strong. He puts his head in the palm of his hand and smiles at me. I sit down beside him and lean my back against the tree.

"Okay, peanut, go for it. I'm all set for my story."

"Well, once upon a time, there was this monkey. The monkey thought it would be nice to have his own trees to climb in. So he went to the store and bought three trees to plant. When he planted the trees, he called one Mama Tree, one Daddy Tree and the other one, the one that was smaller than the other two, he named Baby Tree. The monkey was very good at taking care of the trees. Every day, he went out and watered all three of them. He knew that it would take a long time for the trees to grow into big trees, but that was okay. He didn't mind to wait. Well, one night, a huge, huge storm came. It rained so hard. From inside his house, the monkey watched the trees. They were leaning real bad. Especially Baby Tree. The monkey was scared that it was going to fall over. If it did that, it might not stand back up. The other two bigger trees were doing okay, even though they were swaying a lot, too. The monkey went out in the rain and tied a small stick to the little tree. He was trying to help make it stay straight in the rain. Then the monkey went back inside. He watched it for a little bit, and it seemed to be doing better. It didn't bend so much. So the monkey went to bed.

Well, later that night, when it was real dark and real late, the rain started coming down harder and harder and harder. The stick helped Baby Tree, but the two bigger trees started swaying and bending. They were having a hard time staying up straight. They were scared of falling to the ground and drowning in the rain. Then the big Daddy Tree said to Mama Tree, 'Hey, bend a little toward me and I'll bend a little toward you. That way we'll help keep each other up.' So Daddy Tree bent in a little toward Mama Tree, and Mama Tree bent in a little toward Daddy Tree. Baby Tree was in the middle. At first, this helped everybody out. It kept a lot of the rain off of Baby Tree, and it helped Mama Tree and Daddy Tree from falling. But then the storm got worse and worse. It kept pushing Mama Tree and Daddy Tree in even more. They were starting to lean on Baby Tree. Baby Tree started crying cause it was getting pushed to the ground where all the water was.

Mama Tree said, 'We gotta push ourselves off of Baby Tree.' But Daddy Tree said, 'If we do, we'll all drown.' So they didn't.

The next morning, the monkey came out of his house to see how the trees were. Mama Tree and Daddy Tree were sagging a little, but they were still okay. Baby Tree, though, was smashed. It lay on the ground and couldn't be helped. Mama Tree and Daddy Tree had to use it to help themselves."

Ash's dark eyes looked different than they had at the start of the story. They were a lot darker. After a long time, he shook his head a little and bent it down, but he still didn't say anything. I started feeling a little panicked.

"You don't like it?" I asked, frowning.

If he didn't like it, there was no way I could ever turn it in to my teacher.

Ash lifted his head and smiled a small smile.

"It is a good story, Anna."

His voice was soft.

"I like it. Thank you for sharing it with me. Now, I think you need to share it with your teacher."

"You really do like it?"

"I really, really do. You're a very smart young lady."

That was such a lie that I almost snorted. He laughed softly and looked away from me. Then he looked back and reached out a hand. He touched my arm and nodded.

"You are. Mark my words, that story will get an A."

"Maybe."

"Hey, do you see that bird?" Ash asked me suddenly, pointing up to the sky.

I did not see a bird.

"No. Where?"

"Right there"

"In the tree?"

"No, silly. Right there. See it? Straight up."

I looked. I looked really hard. But I still didn't see a bird.

"You're fooling me. There's no bird."

"There is too. That cloud looks just like a red bird."

I got it now. He loves to make shapes out of clouds. This time, when I looked up, I did see the bird shape in one of the clouds.

"How can something white look like red?" I asked.

Ash sighed heavily and rolled his head sideways to look at me.

"Seriously, Anna, use your imagination. That cloud is red."

"If you say so. It's moving anyway."

"Yeah."

A second's pause.

"Hey, let's follow it," Ash said.

"What?"

Ash was already on his feet.

"Come on, we're going to follow that bird."

I laughed. I liked that game.

"Maybe we'll find its nest," I said.

"That has its three baby birds in it."

"Maybe we'll get to see it pick up a worm to feed its babies."

"I bet there's a crow at its nest and the crow is about to eat the baby birds. We'll get to watch the mama fight away the crow. Did you know there is nothing as dangerous as a mama when she's protecting her babies?"

"That'll be fun," I said.

We were walking through the park. Both me and Ash had our heads tipped back so we could follow the bird cloud. It was really fun. I didn't know where we were going, and I did not care because Ash was with me.

"Hey, our bird is changing!" Ash said suddenly.

I started laughing.

"It's not a bird anymore, Ash! It's a pretzel."

"A *pretzel*? You turned my red bird into a *pretzel*?"

"Well, look at it! It's a pretzel!"

I was laughing so hard. Ash laughed, too, his head still tipped back. Our pretzel bird was now moving slowly just ahead of us. It met up with another cloud. It stuck to the new cloud and changed again.

"Hey, our pretzel just got eaten by an airplane!" Ash said.

"No," I said seriously. "Our pretzel bird just got *on* an airplane. It will help her reach her nest faster. She had to fly a long way away to find food for those babies."

"Ah, well, all the better. She might get back home before the crow gets there."

We were still walking. A minute later, our airplane pretzel bird began to stretch out. It got longer and longer.

"Anna—Anna—"

"It's a—ooph," I said as I ran into someone. I looked up and saw the teenage boy I'd run into. My face got red.

"Sorry," I muttered.

He ignored me and kept walking, but I heard him mutter, "Nutcase."

My heart sinks. I was a nutcase. I was walking backwards with my head tipped up, trying to see where a cloud would go, and laughing because it kept changing shapes. I looked back at Ash. He smiled at me.

"Birds eat nuts."

I laughed.

***** ***** *****

"I see one!" Ash said, with his head tipped back.

He was looking up a real tree this time. After we lost track of our airplane pretzel bird, Ash wanted to go on a hunt for a real bird's nest. He grabbed a huge stick and started walking. It took me a minute longer to find the right kind of stick, and when I finally found one Ash was on up ahead of me. He was so tall. He was so strong. And he was so nice. I really loved him.

I took off running, calling after him to wait up. He did, smiling down at me, and we'd gone off in search of the bird's nest. People passed me and looked at me funny. Ash said they couldn't understand why a pretty little girl like me would want to talk to him. I thought that was dumb. If they knew Ash, they'd want to talk to him, too. I thought they looked at me funny cause every time I thought I saw a bird's nest, I went crazy trying to point it out. Ash would put his hand over his eyes and squint, looking. Then he would say I was seeing things and move on. He wanted to be the one to find the bird's nest. I didn't really care which one of us found one, but I played along and argued that I would find one before he did.

It was all part of the story.

I wasn't really surprised when he called out that he saw a bird's nest.

"Where?" I asked.

He pointed to the top of the huge maple tree he was standing in front of. I tipped my head back to see and, sure enough, I could see just the edge of the nest. It didn't look like a very big bird's nest, but it was definitely a nest. I wondered what was inside it.

"Come on," said Ash, looking towards the tree. He started circling it. The tree forked, and he put a hand around one limb of it.

"Let's climb it and see."

I was surprised when he said he wanted to climb the tree with me so that we could see it better. I wasn't altogether sure that I could climb a tree. I never had before. But I wanted to. I'd always thought it sounded cool to say that you had climbed a tree. And if I climbed one with Ash, I knew it'd be okay cause I knew that Ash wouldn't let anything happen to me.

"Okay."

I walked to stand in front of him.

"Grab hold here," he said, showing me where to put my hand.

"And put your other hand here. You're going to climb on top of that branch there."

My heart was beginning to race. I wasn't real sure I could do this. I reached out and grabbed hold of the branch. Then I pulled my foot up and onto it. I didn't fall. Ash was right behind me, too, waiting for me to climb up so he could climb. I reached for the next branch. Then the next. Then the next. It was getting easier to do the further we went. My heart wasn't racing so much. I felt better and less scared every time I got to a safe branch. I could see the bird's nest real good now.

"We're almost there, Ash!" I said excitedly.

"Great. Keep going."

I did.

A few minutes later, I was sitting on the same thick branch as the bird's nest.

"What's inside it?" Ash asked.

"I can't see it for sure."

"Scoot closer to it."

I grabbed hold of the bark and started inching my way closer to the nest. I told myself not to look down. We had climbed a long way up. I did not want to think about getting down. Ash put his hands on my knees and smiled at me from the branch below me.

"You're fine. Keep scooting."

With his hands on my knees, I wasn't scared hardly at all. I inched closer to the nest until I could finally see over its edge.

"There's three eggs in here, Ash!"

I was real excited. I could see the eggs real good. They were pure white, with no spots or anything. I wondered what kind of birds they were. I wondered where the mother bird was.

Ash wondered the same thing, I guess, cause he said, "Eggs are cool but bad. If the mama bird gets back here, she'll peck our heads off. Come on, let's go back down a branch or two so she'll feel we're safe."

That sounded like a good plan. Except I couldn't get down off the branch I was on. I didn't want to. I was sure I'd miss my footing and fall to the ground. That would be bad. Daddy would kill me if he knew I'd climbed a tree. Girls aren't supposed to do things like that. That made me feel really nervous. I felt my palms start to get sweaty. I wasn't breathing too good, either. *Now*, I was scared.

"Come on, Anna, you can do it. See, watch me."

Ash wrapped one long arm around the tree trunk and swung himself like a monkey onto the branch below him.

"My arms are not monkey arms like yours."

"Monkey arms?" He laughed.

"I'm not as tall as you."

"Kids do this all the time. Come on. You'll be fine."

I scooted until I was laid down on the branch. Then I wrapped both arms around the branch I was lying on and scooted my legs. I scooted them until they fell off. Then I slid down, holding on with both arms, until I felt my feet hit the branch below me. That was good.

Finally, I made it to where Ash was, two branches below the bird's nest.

He sat, legs swinging from the branch, a smile on his face, like always. I scooted up until my back was against the trunk of the tree. That made me feel safer. We weren't that high off the ground anymore, but it was still a nice fall that I didn't want to do.

"You should write a story about that bird."

"There wasn't a bird in the nest," I pointed out.

"Not that bird. The airplane pretzel bird."

I smiled. Then I tipped my head back and looked up toward the nest again.

"What kind of bird do you think those eggs are?"

"Don't know. Wanna sit here until they hatch and we find out?"

I laughed.

"You're silly."

He winked.

"We're pretty high off the ground, aren't we?" I asked.

"Pretty."

"I see the swings from here."

"Yup."

"Those are my favorites."

He was quiet so I didn't say anything else either. After a few minutes, he moved and started climbing down again.

"Where are you going?" I asked.

"To the swings. Race ya there."

By the time I got out of the tree, Ash was running. He wasn't running as fast as I knew he could. He was letting me catch up with him. I ran to where I was walking by his side, and then I slowed down. There were other kids at the playground. I wondered if any of them had a friend as good as Ash. I didn't think they did. I was glad that there were two swings open side by side. Ash got one, and I got the other. He started swinging right away. It took me a little longer to get going. It is still a little hard for me to push myself. But I know how. I just have to make my legs work hard. It wasn't long, though, before I was going just as fast as Ash.

"You're right, Anna—this is fun," Ash said from the swing beside me.

I barely heard him.

I love the swings. When I get going really fast, like I am right now, I can feel the cool wind across my face. It feels good, even though I usually don't like cold things. I like the way it blows the hair off my neck. I pump my legs real hard to make me go faster. I pull my arms out and then back, my legs in, then out again. It feels good to work my arms and legs like this. I turn my head to the side to look at Ash. He is swinging fast, too, but I am going faster now. He still has his little smile on his face. That makes me happy.

After a while, swinging gets a little hard and I slow myself down. Ash does, too.

"Hey, you ready for a break?" he asked.

It is getting a little darker. The sun is not so high in the sky now. And I am getting tired. I nod. Me and Ash walk back towards the garden, the one that has the big tree we like so much. When we get there, we both lay on our backs and stare up at the sky. There are white lines from airplanes flying across and a few puffy clouds right above us. None of them look like anything, really, though.

I yawn.

I am getting sleepy.

It has been a lot of fun playing with Ash today, though. And I am super glad that he liked my story.

"Ash?"

"Yeah?"

"I don't want to go home."

He didn't answer me.

I looked over at him, but he was still looking at the sky. When he did look at me, he smiled a little.

"Here you go," he said.

He stretched his arm out. I lifted my head and he put his arm under it. It was nice to lay on his arm. I knew that nothing was going to hurt me right now cause Ash was here. I wanted Ash to go with me everywhere. I loved him a lot. He was my best friend. It is hard when there is not a place at home where I can feel really, really safe.

I closed my eyes and yawned again.

"Anna Peanut?"

"Hm?"

"I think it's time you got home, before your mama starts lookin' for you."

He was right, of course. But I didn't want to go home. I didn't want to. If Mama got worried, though, Daddy would hear about it. It had been a perfect day. I didn't want that to change when I got home. I sat up.

"Okay."

"Come on, I'll walk you back."

And he did. We didn't talk a lot on the way home. I was just thinking about the airplane pretzel bird, the ice cream, the bird's nest, and the swing. I was thinking how glad I was that Ash is my friend. When we saw my house, I just turned to him and wrapped both my arms around his waist in a hug. Ash put both arms around me, too. It felt really good. Nobody gave me hugs like Ash did. His hugs always made me feel like I was loved.

"See ya later," I said.

"Ecrivez-moi, peanut."

***** ***** *****

Birds were chirping outside my window. I smelled bacon and biscuits cooking. My back hurt. I opened my eyes and looked down. Why was I at my desk? I must have fallen asleep and slept most of the night at my desk. I looked down. My story notebook was open. I rubbed my eyes and stretched. Then I looked down at the story notebook again.

> *"Hey, our bird is changing!" Ash said suddenly.*
> *I started laughing.*
> *"It's not a bird anymore, Ash! It's a pretzel."*
> *"A pretzel? You turned my red bird into a pretzel?"*
> *"Well, look at it! It's a pretzel!"*
> *I was laughing so hard. Ash laughed, too, his head still tipped back. Our pretzel bird was now moving slowly just ahead of us. It met up with another cloud. It stuck to the new cloud and changed again.*
> *"Hey, our pretzel just got eaten by an airplane!"*

I'd been reading the story of me and Ash at the park. I smiled and closed the story notebook. Maybe that's why I did not dream of Daddy last night.

It was time to get ready for church.

6
The Fifth Commandment

What Would Jesus Do?

The kids in my Sunday School class wear these bracelets that say that. The bracelets come in all different colors. One day, I didn't see anyone wearing them and then it was, like, the very next day, ten of the kids in my class had them on. The first thing I thought when I saw them was, "About what?" But then I understood. The bracelets are cool looking—they have a rough feel to them. I think they're made of rubber or something, and the words are written in black. Some of the kids in my Sunday School class don't wear them on their wrists—they have them attached to the zipper of their bags or purses. Some of the kids wear more than one. I want one. But Mama says that we shouldn't need a reminder to follow Jesus. We should learn to think like He does without having to look at our wrists for a reminder. That's what she says. So I don't have one. But I want one.

Sunday School class is not really my favorite place to be. If the kids at my school come from a different country, the kids in my Sunday School class come from a different *solar system* than me. I mean, the kids at school seem okay and everything but the kids at church always seem so *happy.* They are always laughing and always smiling and always talking. The kids at school talk and smile and laugh, too—but not as much. Plus, the kids in church are always dressed real nice. Mama says it's disrespectful to God for girls not to wear dresses or skirts in church. I am not allowed to wear pants, even nice pants, to church, no matter how many times I ask. Mama says we gotta dress up for God; sometimes I think we dress up for the other people in church. But I always go along. I always put a dress on and brush my hair real pretty. We don't go to church *every* week; it's usually just when Mama didn't have to work the night before, or when Easter comes around. Maybe that's part of the reason I don't like going: because I don't really know the kids. I just see them every few weeks and when I do see them, they always seem like they are the happiest people in the world. It makes me feel like I'm weird. I'm not real sad or anything, but I don't laugh all the time either.

Suddenly, we hear Mrs. Hapsburg, our teacher, clap three times. I look toward her and clap three times, too. That's the rule. When she claps, we have to stop, be quiet and clap three times. It's to get our attention.

"Please take a seat."

I was already in my seat. The other kids were playing in centers, with the blocks or the puzzles. I didn't have anyone to play with, though, and I didn't want to do something stupid in church. That's why I just sat most of the time. I usually had my story notebook with me, but I forgot it this morning cause we were in a hurry.

"Someone tell me something that your mom or dad told you to do this morning?"

At first, no one raised their hand. Raising your hand is not cool. It means you are the teacher's pet. But I like teachers. I know that's weird since I'm not a good student, but I do. But I didn't like this question. It made me think of Daddy. So I didn't raise my hand. A black kid—I couldn't remember his name—raised his hand first.

"To hurry up."

"To hurry up? That's a good one. I bet several of us heard that this morning. What else? Anyone's mom or dad tell them to do something else this morning?"

"To get my offering," another girl said.

"To stop making noises at breakfast," Wes said.

I like Wes.

"What kind of noises were you making?" another kid asked.

Wes put one hand under the opposite arm and made a funny noise. Mrs. Hapsburg tipped her head.

"I imagine that your mother did not like that. I don't either."

Wes stopped.

I couldn't think of anything that Mama told me to do this morning. I was already dressed. She didn't tell me to eat my breakfast or to hurry up. She didn't tell me to get my offering. She didn't tell me to do anything, except have a good time in class, which I was trying to do. But Daddy. All of a sudden, I had this picture in my mind of something that happened last night, when he came to my room. He asked me to do something that I didn't want to do. He said he'd asked nicely and he didn't want to have to ask again.

"Now, my next question is one you do not have to answer, but I want you to think of the answer. Did you do what your mom or dad told you to do? Did you hurry up? Did you get your offering? Did you stop making noises at breakfast? Did you obey your parents?"

She paused for a moment to allow us to think about the answer. I did. I always obey.

"The Bible tells us that we are supposed to honor our parents. One way that we honor them is by obeying them. Why do you think obeying our parents is important?"

"Cause they're smarter than we are."

"No they're not. They're just *older*."

"They are too smarter than us. They know stuff that we don't know."

"Only cause they don't tell us those things."

"They keep us from getting hurt. Like, making us ride our bikes with a helmet in case we fall off. We wouldn't think about that, usually. We'd just want to ride the bike. But they have to look out for us. I mean, that's what parents are for, right?"

Ms. Hapsburg smiled.

"That's partly right. Part of a parent's job is to ensure the safety of their kids. Part of it is to ensure their emotional safety, too: that they are loved and played with and supported, that sort of thing. Okay, so we think that part of the reason we're supposed to obey our parents is because they are older and maybe smarter. Why else?"

Silence.

Ms. Hapsburg looked at me and raised her brows. I dropped my eyes to the table. I didn't like this lesson and I was not going to participate.

"Anna?"

Shoot.

"Anna, why do you think we should obey our parents?"

I shrug.

"I dunno."

"Can you think of just one reason?"

I sighed.

"I do it cause I'm just s'posed to. I mean, they're my parents. I gotta obey them."

She tipped her head.

"How many of you ever think about questioning the authority of your parents? Anyone?"

"You mean, how many of us disobey them?"

She nodded.

"Have you ever been forbidden to do something, but done it anyway?"

No one said anything, so Ms. Hapsburg told us her story.

"I did. One time, there was this party at my friend's house. I was a little older than you guys, but not a whole lot. And I really wanted to go to the party. But my friend's mom was going to be out of town and so my parents told me that I could not go to the party. I went anyway. It was a horrible experience and I ended up in a car with a fifteen-year-old drunk driver. We crashed, and she was hurt pretty bad. I wasn't, thankfully, but I could have been. My parents knew what kind of party was likely going to take place and they didn't want me to be put in a position where I could be hurt. All I wanted was to have a good time with my friends. After that, I obeyed my parents because I trusted them and their judgment. If they told me that I could not do something, then I trusted that they had a good reason for telling me no. Sometimes I argued the point, sometimes I didn't think it was fair. But I always trusted what they told me. Anyone want to take a guess why I trusted them?"

"Because they were right about the party?"

She shook her head.

"No. I trusted them because I loved them. I love my mom very much. I love my dad very much. And it hurts them and it makes them sad and it makes them have a bad day when their daughter deliberately disobeys them. Disobeying is a form of disrespect. It tells the parent that you don't care enough about them to do as they asked. That's why we have to obey God. I try to obey God because I want Him to know that I love Him and that I trust Him. It's not always easy, but it is always the right thing to do."

"Parents can be wrong."

"Sometimes, yes, they can be. But that's not the point. The point isn't really whether they have a valid reason for telling you not to do something. The party could have been perfectly harmless. Parents can sometimes be over protective. But, when it comes right down to it, the point isn't the parent: the point is whether or not you are going to show the parent that you love him or her. The point is you: you have the opportunity, every time your parent tells you to do something, to show trust and love and respect or not to. If you trust and obey your parents, then when you get all grown up and don't have them to tell you what to do anymore, it will be easier for you to trust and obey the rules that God gives us through the Bible. You may not always agree with your parents but even when you disagree with them, you still love them. You may not always agree with God, either. But you need to always trust Him and believe in Him, and the best way to do that is to simply make a decision that you will obey His rules."

I wanted out of this class. I sat there listening to her talk for a few more minutes, but all I could think about was getting out. I heard the kids make a few more comments but I sort of stopped listening after the bit about love and trust and all that. She said we had to make a decision to show our parents we loved them. With my mom, that was easy. But... Do I love Daddy? Yes. I do.

And so I obey.

***** ***** *****

It wasn't raining today. This was big news. It has rained almost every day for the past week or more. Everybody was getting sick of it. My mom kept saying that people at work talked about it all night. Mama kept asking me where I wanted to go. Did I want to go to the library? Did I want to go to the science center? We could go skating. Did I want to go window shopping? The thing is— I don't really want to go anywhere. I just want to stay home all day. I just want to stay in my room. I have an iPod shuffle. It's great. It's even engraved with my name on the back of it, and it's pink, my favorite color. All I want to do is stay in my room and listen to it or read a book or something. Mama says it's important to get out of the house. She says it's important to get out of my room. So I

94

can either go somewhere with her, or I can at least help her cook dinner. I guess I can help cook.

I kind of like cooking. I like the kitchen. It feels like where I'm s'posed to be. Mama says that means that maybe one day I'll be a famous chef. That would be neat. We are cooking spaghetti and rolls. She lets me break the noodles and drop them in the boiling water. She'll let me stir it, too. I watch the steam rise from the pot. Even though it is really hot, I kind of like sticking my face over the steam for a few seconds. It is hard to think when things are so hot and I like not being able to think.

"Damn it!" Daddy curses, slamming the front door shut.

He storms into the kitchen.

"What's wrong?" Mama asks.

"I don't have anymore of the right screws. I'll have to go to Lowe's."

Mama says nothing as Daddy grabs his wallet from the counter and walks out of the house again. Mama is buttering the rolls. They are about to go into the oven.

"What's he making?" I ask.

Mama sighs heavily and shakes her head.

"I don't know. He's been working on something for the past few nights. I will be glad when it's done, whatever it is."

Me too.

When Daddy gets mad from working with the wood, I am the one who almost always knows the most about it.

"How was class?" Mama asks.

I shrug.

"Okay."

I don't want to talk about Sunday School. I did not like the lesson. She will ask more about it if I don't say something else. I think of something else to talk about.

"I have to write a story for school about a tree."

"A tree? What does the tree have to do?"

"Whatever we want it to do."

"Do you remember *The Giving Tree*?"

I smile and nod my head as I use the wooden spatula to stir the spaghetti noodles.

"I used to read that to you every single night. I bet you heard it at least a hundred times."

"I liked it."

"Me too."

The Giving Tree is a really good book. It's for kids, but it's still good. It's about this tree that is friends with this boy. The boy keeps wanting things and the tree gives the boy it's bark, it's leaves, even it's wood. In the end, the boy and the tree get old and the boy just wants to sit on the tree stump. It's a good story. I like it. I probably won't be able to come up with a good story about a tree like that one. I look down at the pot again and see the bubbles boiling in the water. I wonder how hot it would be, touching something hot might sting a little but that's probably all it would do—

"Anna!"

Mama's loud shriek makes me jerk my hand back.

"What are you doing? *Never* put your hand into a boiling pot."

My heart is racing and I'm shaking a little.

I really didn't know I'd stretched out my hand towards the pot.

Mama must see something funny on my face.

"Go on, I've got this. Why don't you go watch a show or something?"

"Okay," I mumble and walk quickly out of the kitchen, with my head hung low.

I still wondered what the boiling water might have done to my finger.

"Knock, knock."

I look up from my desk, where I am trying to start writing the tree story. I told Ash I'd have it for him to read soon. Mama has not left for work yet so I am surprised when Daddy opens the bedroom door.

"Hey, peaches," he says lightly.

"Hi."

Daddy comes into the room.

"I've got something for you."

He reaches outside the bedroom door and pulls something in. It is two separate shelves. They have a pretty design on the front of them. They are maple, which is my favorite kind of wood. I smile weakly.

"They're great."

"I'll hang them up for you and you can use them to put your books on. It won't be enough, but I'll make you a bigger bookcase later. Maybe you can put your favorites on these so they'll always be easy for you to find."

Again, I smile weakly.

"Thank you," I mumble.

My teeth are clenched and the smile is hard. I don't want a present.

"Do you like them?" Daddy asks, his blue eyes bright, his smile wide.

He is happy that he made them for me, and that he did a good job. He looks like a little kid in a candy store. I feel like I am the grown-up. My heart hurts as I nod my head a little.

"Sure do."

"Great. I went ahead and brought up some nails and the hammer. It'll just take a minute for me to hang 'em up."

He looks around my room. It is pretty and pink and frilly. Mama likes a lot of lace. My bed is made, as always, and has my three favorite stuffed animals—a bear named Puddin, a dog named Applesauce, and an elephant named Ears—laying on the pillows. Everything is neat. The walls have framed pictures of me and some of me with Mama. That's all. No posters, nothing like that. Mama redecorates my room every few years. Sometimes she'll ask me what I want, sometimes she just comes in and does it for me. It's nice to have the room changed every once in awhile.

Daddy finds a spot for the two shelves near my short bookcase and starts hammering. I look away. I really don't want the shelves up. But I can't tell him that.

Finally, they are hung up. He comes over and gives me a hug and then nods.

"See ya later," he says and then walks out.

I look over my shoulder at the shelves. Then I look back down at my story notebook. I don't want to put books on the new shelves. I will wait and do that later.

I can't think of what to write in my story. The page is still blank. I keep thinking about those shelves, and how I don't want them hung up. It is my room. He didn't even ask me if I wanted him to hang them up. Tonight, he will come in my room. I know it. And he will tell me that he made the shelves for me, and how I should give him something. He might even ask me to tell him what I want to give him. My heart starts racing a little. It is getting hard to breathe. He gives me presents all the time. But I don't want them. I don't want presents.

Before I know what I am doing, I get up and I take the shelves down off the walls, the highest one first, then the second one. I drag them to my closet and I put them in it. I feel better now. Maybe I will tell him that one fell down and so I just took the other one down, too. Maybe he won't notice. Maybe I am a bad daughter. I grab my story notebook and pencil and move to sit on the bed. I lay down and open up the story notebook again. I need to write a story for Ash. A story about a tree. It is hard to think about anything but the shelves. Finally my hand starts moving across the paper.

I don't know how long I write. My hand has started hurting a little and my fingers ache some when Mama comes in to tell me goodnight. She is leaving for work. I should put away the story notebook now and get ready for bed. But I don't want to. I want to finish the story. I think Ash will like reading about it. My teacher might, too. I put my pen down and stretch my fingers real hard; then I start writing again. It is really dark outside my window, but I don't care.

Creak.

My pen freezes. I know that creak. It is the sound that happens on the third step away from outside my room. Daddy is coming. I only have a minute. I don't have enough time to get in bed. So I just keep my head down and try to keep my pen moving, even though it's really hard to think about the story now.

He does not knock now. He just comes in. He is not smiling.

"I asked your Mama if you'd gotten your books put on your shelves yet. She said that they weren't up."

His tone is not happy. I swallow hard. Before I can say anything, Daddy jerks my closet door open. I don't know how he knew they were in there. He pulls out one of the shelves and then takes two steps toward me. I scramble out of my chair and start backing up towards the window, but he leans over and grabs my wrist.

"Young lady, you look at this shelf. Look at it, goddammit!"

My eyes move to the shelf.

"Do you have any idea how long it took me to make these? Do you know how hard it is to build something out of wood?"

I try to answer but can't. He drops the shelf and hits me hard across the face. I land on the ground and try to curl my legs up to my face. *Honor thy mother and thy father, Exodus 20:12. Honor thy mother and thy father, Exodus 20:12.* That's what I think. Screaming will just make him madder. I look up just in time to see him pull his belt from his pants. He can always tell Mama he had to spank me for something. His arm is raised and it comes down—it burns really bad and I scream out.

"Get up, Anna."

Daddy sounds like he is in water. He sounds like he is really far away. I cannot get up. I try but when I move my legs to stand, they fall back down.

"No? You don't want to get up?" Daddy asks. "Fine."

I see him undo his pants and I close my eyes. I don't want to be here. I want to be anywhere else. Daddy falls on top of me. I can feel him. He is hot. He is very heavy, and it is really hard to breathe again. I feel like I'm about to get sick. The floor is very hard beneath me. I can feel the carpet. All of a sudden, I am really tired. Really, really tired. I just give up. I stop fighting. I stop crying. I just lay there. I stare at the ceiling. I wish I was in my bed so I could see the crack. But I'm not. I think about Ash. I think about his smile. He has the best smile. It is so warm and so happy. He has a happy face. He laughs a lot, too. And his eyes are so kind. I have never seen anyone with a face like Ash's.

Honor thy father and thy mother, Exodus 20:12. That was our memory verse from this morning. We have to obey. That's what God says. Fighting is not obeying. Maybe Daddy doesn't know I love him. Maybe I really did

100

do something wrong. He had worked hard on those shelves and I wasn't really nice about them. Maybe if I had been nice. Maybe if I had just left the shelves alone, and put books on them. When someone gives you a present, you're supposed to be nice about it. I bet Ash was always nice to his mommy and daddy, and if they gave him a present, he didn't put it away. I really need to see Ash. I really want to. This hurts a lot. But Ash isn't here.

Daddy falls off of me and gets up. He takes the shelves and hangs them back up.

"Put books on them," he says and then grabs his pants and walks out of my bedroom.

I just lay on the floor. Suddenly, I start shaking. I am super cold. And I wish I was not alone. When I am alone, all I can think about is what just happened. It was my fault. I know it was. But it still hurts. I hold my hand out, the way Ash once told me to. "Dear Father, please hold my hand," I whisper. It takes a few minutes but, after a while, I stop shaking so bad and there is a heat that comes over my hand. It feels like a rush of hot air running over my palm. And then the strangest thing happens. I hear a quiet whisper, a really, really soft whisper say gently, "I love you."

I start crying all over again.

7
The Gift

Most grown-ups think that the only thing kids think about is school and friends. I mean, I guess parents know what kind of music their kids like to listen to and what TV shows their kids watch. Some of them may know if the kids have something that they are really good at, like playing a sport or doing something with music. I guess that's why some kids in my class are in the chorus—cause their parents know the kids like it enough to pay for instruments and schedule the practices and all. Even those parents, though, the ones that know what kinds of stuff their kids like, don't know that the kids think about lots of stuff they ain't never gonna tell anybody else.

Take me, for example.

Sure, I think about school a lot. I mean, I spend, like, most of my day five days a week there, and I'm usually pretty upset about failing another stinking math test. For a lot of kids, failing a test isn't a big deal; to me, though, it's a huge deal. So, yeah, I think about school. But I also think about other stuff. Today, I can't stop thinking about earthquakes. Our teacher told us that the earth, like, really moves. She said that it sits on two plates and that they move and that that is what causes an earthquake. I thought this was so interesting that I can't stop thinking about it. She said that it doesn't have to move much to create the worst damage—just the smallest movement and we call it a catastrophe. California must sit right on the edge of the plate or something because they have all kinds of earthquakes. Just after Christmas last year, they had a really big one and people are still there, helping to rebuild it and clean up and stuff. Eighteen days after it happened, they were still pulling people from debris. Eighteen days trapped under really heavy stuff. That would be terrible. The cool part is that some of the people they pulled out from the rubble eighteen days after the earthquake were still alive. One girl was hurt really bad; I don't remember why, exactly (other than there was probably a building on top of her for eighteen days) but they didn't know if she was going to live or not. She had to be flown to a special hospital in a different state. I don't know if she lived or not in the end. Some guy, though, who was pulled free the same day as the girl, wasn't hurt at all. I think he had to go to the hospital too, but just to make sure nothing was broken or anything like that. He was probably really hungry and tired, too, but he wasn't *really* hurt, not like the girl.

Sometimes I think about that, about how two people can go through the same thing and turn out completely different. This morning, when I was eating breakfast, Mama was watching the news. Sometime during the night, this fifteen-year-old girl called 911 and said she couldn't take what her dad was doing to her no more. She told them that she had a gun and she was going to use it if he came into her room again. By the time the police got there, she had used the gun. But not on her dad. She killed herself instead. I stopped eating. I couldn't even remember what kind of cereal was in my bowl. I just kept wanting to hear more about the girl. When Mama realized that I was actually watching the story, she turned it off, of course, so I didn't get to hear the details or anything. But all day I've been thinking about that girl. All I can think about was that she was fifteen—only five years older than me.

***** ***** *****

"What'cha thinking about?" Ash asked, leaning against the trunk of the tree.

103

He came over to my house most days now. We liked to hang out in the backyard, under the maple tree. I was afraid to ask Mama and Daddy if he could come in the house. I knew Mama wouldn't really like me talking to a grown-up man all the time. But the more I saw Ash, the more I liked him. He was my best friend, and I loved hanging out with him.

I shrugged.

"Don't know."

"How was school today?"

"Okay."

Ash arched his brows, turned the corners of his lips down and nodded. He didn't say anything for a few minutes before he sat down beside me, bending one of his legs up like he always does.

"Story game."

I smiled, looking over at him. He has really dark brown eyes that are super pretty. The girls in my school all think Clay Hughes is cute, but Clay Hughes has nothing on my Ash. Even better, I love the story game. It makes me laugh all the time.

"You start," I said.

"Once upon a time, there was a little boy named Alex and one day…"

"One day, he went for a walk in the park. He was playing the game where you can't step on any cracks. He was picking up his shoe to step over one of the cracks in the sidewalk when…"

"When a bee stung him in the ankle."

I laughed.

"Yeah. And it hurt real bad. His foot fell to the ground and stepped right on the crack."

"But he didn't think about it, then, because the bee sting was hurting him. He started trying to walk to the bench, so he could sit down. When he got to the bench, he..."

"Sat down and pulled up the bottom of his pants a little so he could see where the bee had stung him. It was real red. He was scared cause he thought the stinger might still be in him so he leaned over to get a good look at it when..."

"He lost his balance..."

"Cause a pigeon landed on his head."

It was Ash's turn to laugh. His eyes lit up as he continued the story.

"Right. A pigeon flew on his head and made him lose his balance, and he fell. But not onto the ground—he fell into the water where there were bunches of ducks trying to eat pieces of bread thrown in by kids."

"Eeeww, yuck," I said, picturing the water at the park I like to visit. "Alex could swim, though, so he started swimming fast as he could, trying to get to the water's edge," I continued.

"It was hard going, though, because the ducks thought he was food and started pecking him. First his arms, then his legs."

"And he kept screaming, but no one was at the park that day."

"Then he came up with a great idea! He thought that if the ducks thought he was a duck, they'd leave him alone. So he started quacking and swimming real slow. It worked! The ducks didn't peck him so much anymore."

"Finally, he made it to the water's edge and pulled himself up onto the dry land. When he was there, he laid there. He was really cold. All of a sudden..."

"He heard a buzzing sound above him and he thought, 'oh no!' The bee is back!"

I laughed at the horrified look on Ash's face and piped in, "And he started begging the bee not to sting him again. And then the bee started laughing."

"The bee buzzed down in front of Alex's face, and Alex just knew the bee was going to sting him in the nose…"

"Or the eye!"

"Or the eye. But the bee didn't. Instead, he just laughed and laughed. The bee was still laughing when Alex got up and started running away but, before he got too far, the bee said, 'Don't step on no more cracks!'"

I smiled and shook my head. Ash was always the one who could tie the end of the story to the start of the story. I had a hard time doing that. The story game was meant to be silly. Usually, it was a lot funnier than that story. But it made me smile, and I was happy about that. That's one of the things I love about Ash: he can always make me smile, even when I don't think I can.

A red bird flew in front of us and Ash grinned, turning his head to watch it.

"Did you know that red birds are good luck for real?"

"That's what Mama says."

"She's right. You don't see one a lot so whenever you do, it's supposed to bring you good luck."

"Do you believe in luck, Ash?"

Ash shrugged. He paused a minute to think about it and then shrugged a second time.

"I don't know. Do you?"

The screen door to our back door opened and Daddy stuck his head out.

"Anna? Come on in."

I felt my heart fall. Ash watched me quietly and then he smiled at me.

"I forgot to tell you something about our boy Alex."

"What's that?"

"He was wearing purple polka dot pants."

I laughed and stood.

106

"And an orange striped shirt."

Ash's laugh is worth a million dollars, it's so pretty. I wanted to say something to make him laugh harder, but I'm not funny. So I just smiled at him as I stood up, ready to go inside now.

"Bye, Ash."

"Ecrivez-moi, Anna."

I started walking towards the front door, but then I stopped and looked back over at him.

"Ash?"

"Yes?"

"Do *you* believe in wishes and luck and all that?"

He took a deep breath and nodded his head slowly.

"Why, yes. I believe I do. What about you?"

I frowned as Daddy called my name again. He was going to get angry pretty soon.

I started moving my feet towards the house and said softly, "No. I don't."

But I want to.

***** ***** *****

Three and a half steps from the top of the stairs, the floor creaks. If I concentrate real hard and lift my head off the pillow just a little, I can hear it from within my bedroom even with the door closed. I have been laying in bed for an hour now, thinking about which is best: acting asleep even though I know he'll know I'm not or getting up and trying to read something, maybe write down the stories that I've heard from Ash today. In the end, I decide to just lay there. It doesn't really matter what I'm doing.

My eyes watch in the dark as the knob on my bedroom door turns a little, slowly. I always wonder why he opens the door slowly, especially on nights like tonight when there's no reason to rush, since Mama is at work. I

107

don't mean to, but I find myself holding my breath and my eyes stay glued to the door. Daddy walks in a second later. At first, I don't notice that he has something in his hands. All I notice is that he doesn't have a shirt on. That's probably not a good sign. Definitely not.

"Anna?" he asks.

It's when he starts walking towards me that I notice that he has something in his right hand. It is a magazine. I wonder why he has a magazine with him. He doesn't want me to read with him, does he?

"Hi."

My voice is paper thin.

He reaches out to the night table beside me and turns on the lamp. Light floods the room and I squint my eyes, trying hard to adjust to the brightness. Part of me is scared to look away from him, but I can't help it: my head rolls to the side, away from the brightness of the light.

"I have something to show you. Sit up."

It takes me a few minutes to respond. I am scared. I don't know what he wants to show me, and it makes me nervous. I know it can't be good.

The bed dips when he sits down beside my legs. I am glad that the blanket is pulled up over me so that my legs don't touch his. Yet. He hands me the magazine. It is *Vogue*.

"Your mother was looking through that earlier, before she went to work. Go ahead, look in it."

On the cover was a picture of Julia Roberts, her big lips turned into a pucker, her hand held straight out under her mouth. Blowing a kiss. I liked Julia Roberts. She wasn't only pretty, but she seemed really nice. I kind of liked her crazy, loud laugh, too. It made her seem more like me or my mom than some of the other models who always looked and acted and seemed so perfect. I opened it up and started flipping the pages. I didn't know what I was looking

108

for. I didn't know what I was supposed to find. There were the pages of advertisements, trying to sell me a brand of Taylor Swift cosmetics, which I'm not allowed to wear until I'm sixteen. There was a page advertising the latest model Ford.

"Do you see somebody you think is pretty?" Daddy asked.

I frown. I didn't like the question. It made me that much more scared. Daddy doesn't just ask questions for no reason. I didn't know what the reason for this one was, but I knew it was bad. I just shrugged my shoulders, making sure to keep my eyes on the magazine.

"Nobody?" he asked. "Come on, tell me who you think is pretty. This is a game your mother and I play. She thinks she's pretty, Cindy Crawford," he said, pointing to a picture of Cindy Crawford smiling wide. "What about you?"

I said nothing, but turned the page in the magazine again. I was upon the cover story now, the one about Julia Roberts. There were multiple photographs of her. There she was with big black sunglasses and a brown child in her arms, another one hanging onto her hand.

Finally, cause I knew he was going to make me give him an answer, I said, "She's pretty," pointing to the big picture of Julia, sitting on a white sofa, dressed in a short black dress, her hair pulled back into a fancy bun, tendrils of red curling around her face. She *was* beautiful.

Having given my answer, I looked back at Daddy, hoping that was all I had to do. He took the magazine away from me and looked at Julia Roberts for a minute before he nodded, arching his brows. He then turned and put the magazine on the night table. Then he turned back to me and reached out. I didn't mean to, honest, but I flinched when his hand came toward my face. I got scared, then, cause that usually makes him mad. But he didn't seem to get mad this time. He just used his hand to touch my cheek and then brushed my hair away from my face.

"You know what, Anna?"

I couldn't answer. I tried. But I couldn't. My body was rigid now: in less than a minute, it had grown tight as a bowstring. Right behind my forehead, a terrible headache made my eyes hurt and it made my head feel as though it were quivering back and forth. I didn't really know it all at the time, though. All I could think about was the moment, what I needed to do right that second. I needed to give a response. Good girls never ignored their parents. Somehow, I managed to shake my head.

He smiled. Daddy is cute. Some of the kids at school have told me that, when they see him pick me up. He's got a crooked smile, it slants up at the corner, and there's a small space between his bottom front two teeth. There's also a speck of white in his right eye. He has blue eyes. His hands are smooth even though he works with wood, making all kinds of different things. He can seem quite gentle.

"I didn't choose Julia Roberts. I didn't choose Cindy Crawford, either. You want to know who I chose?"

He leaned forward and put his lips against my cheek. I closed my eyes and swallowed hard, feeling my stomach pitch itself forward and then drop.

"I chose you. You're my chosen beauty."

His hand is moving. I squeeze my eyes, and my legs, tightly closed.

The next thing I remember is the salty taste of the tear as it slipped into the corner of my mouth. I hear him grunting. I feel my body shaking. I know what's happening, but, then again, I don't, cause I'm just not there. It feels like I am somewhere in the air, watching it happen. I see it, but the only thing I feel is the taste of my tears. Then I hear a tiny voice saying, "You're hurting me," and I realize that

that voice is mine. I feel like I have to scream. If I don't scream, I'm going to burst. Panic is rising in my chest now, I feel it, like a bubble of vomit stuck in my throat. I really have to scream. I bite my tongue, which makes me cry harder. I bite it again so that I don't scream. Daddy hates it when I scream. Just before the scream comes out, everything stops. My body isn't being shook like popcorn anymore, even the sound of his breathing is fading. I feel the hard thing go away and then a rush of cold air hits my sweating skin as he finally stands up off the bed. The bubble, holding the scream, starts to go away and there's suddenly more air in the room for me to breathe again. I don't have to scream anymore.

I just stare above me. There is the crack on my ceiling that I like to look at.

My body hurts. My privates hurt, and itch, too. I need to take a bath. Maybe in a little while, when I am sure he is asleep, I will be able to do that. Maybe I will just need to wait until my mom comes home from work. The tears have stopped now, and I distantly hear him tell me goodnight and open my bedroom door. A moment later, I hear it click and know without looking that the door is closed again. Suddenly, a picture of Ash swims above my head. I see him sitting against the maple tree, his eyes closed, a book in his hands. I see him in the Book Trunk, smiling as he tells me a story. What would he say if he saw me like this? What would he tell me to do? Without warning, my eyes sting with more tears. Breathing is hard. It hurts, but I roll over to my side, grabbing the edge of the blanket with my fingers and pulling it up higher around my neck. I don't want anyone to see me again, not ever. Not even Ash.

***** ***** *****

Morning comes way too fast. I am still really sleepy. My head feels like a volcano again. I don't think I can get up. I really don't want to go to school today. I just want to stay in bed and never have to see anyone. It's not like I'm smart or anything, anyway. Then I hear my mom downstairs making breakfast. If I don't get up pretty soon, she'll come in my room to see what's wrong. She might even try and take my temperature. A headache might let me stay home but, even if it did, I'd have Mama coming in every ten minutes to see if I was okay. It'd be better, and easier, to go to school.

When I get up and start to pull on my clothes, I notice there is a bruise on my leg. I don't know how that happened. I quickly look away from it and keep getting dressed. My mission now is to get out of the house without seeing Daddy. Of course, none of my prayers are answered: he is sitting at the table already when I get to the kitchen. He smiles at me and then looks back at his newspaper.

"Good morning, Anna."

"'Morning," I mutter.

"You want orange juice, Anna?" Mama asks.

I nod.

"Yes, ma'am."

She fixes me a glass and puts it down in front of me at the table. It is hard to sit down so I wait to do so until she turns her back. *No questions, please God.*

Thankfully, breakfast is ready and I eat in a hurry. When my mom gets up to clear away the dishes, I get up and say I'm going to go on out and wait for the bus. Mama gives me a hug and I can't help but smile as I smell her familiar scent. Somehow, no matter what she's doing, Mama always smells of lilac soap. I don't tell Daddy bye. Then again, he doesn't tell me bye, either.

When I get on the bus, I get out my notebook. I can hear the other kids talking and laughing, but I try not to listen to what they are saying. I just get out my notebook. I mean to write about the story game me and Ash played yesterday but, before I know what's happening, I am writing about what happened last night.

"It's like I'm having a nightmare. I can see it and I can hear it—but I can't really feel it. The only part I can feel is the sticking part and that only lasts a minute or two. The rest of it, I don't feel. That makes me sad. It worries me. People are supposed to feel when something bad is happening to them. They are supposed to feel sad, but I didn't last night, not when it was happening. I think it means I am broken."

I don't know what made me write that. Usually, I only write down the stories. I read it. It's true, though. I have to be broken if I can't feel something like that when it's happening. It can't be normal to feel—nothing—when you're being hurt real bad. Maybe it was all just a nightmare. Maybe it didn't really happen at all. It would be easy to convince myself of that, except that every time I walk my legs and privates still hurt a little, they're still sore. It happened. I just wish it didn't.

"Anna?"

Startled, I look up. A few of the cool girls are snickering at me as they walk past my seat on the bus. The bus driver is looking at me with a funny expression on his face, as though he's waiting for me to get up. I didn't even know we were already at the school. I jerk into action, flipping closed the story notebook so fast I feel a little bit of wind hit me in the face.

***** ***** *****

School is dumb. Math is even dumber. I mean, I am *never* going to read word problems like the ones on this test and have to figure out how many miles Sue travels in an hour if she's going seventy miles an hour. All I *might* need to know is when Sue would get where she's going, and if I needed to know that, Sue could tell me, cause she'd have a cell phone with her. It's just dumb. Or, I guess, maybe it's just me that's dumb. The other kids don't seem to be so stumped: they are all writing something at least. I don't even know where to start. It's not that I don't listen in class, cause I do, even when it's really hard. It's not that I don't ever turn in my homework, cause I do, and it's always completed. I just don't know the answers, or understand my teacher when she is trying to explain it to me. It's like she's talking in a whole other language that I've never heard before. I stare at her working problems on the board all day long and, when I'm watching her, I think I can try it. But when I get home and start work on my math homework, I have no idea what she was talking about or where to start. Like I said, I'm just dumb. I can feel the heat rush to my face—it is turning red now as I stare at the problems. Most of the other kids have already turned in their tests. The teacher's grading them now. I start scribbling numbers in the margins of my paper. Finally, I come up with something that *could* be the answer and leave it.

I'm done. I go up and hand in my paper.

Luckily, she won't have mine graded before the bell rings—there's only another minute of class left. Then school will be out and I can go home. Anyplace is better than staring at a bunch of numbers, feeling like I can't even count right. Sometimes it's hard for me to believe I'm ten.

The bell rings and I quickly gather up my books and walk out of the class, ahead of the other kids who are loudly talking to their friends now. I hear snitches of their conversations and wonder what it would be like to be a part of one. As soon as the bell rings, it's like we've all just been let out of a zoo—so many kids running and walking and talking, trying to make it outside to their bus on time. I'm one of them—and yet, I'm not. Except that I am glad that school is over.

I decide not to take the bus home today. It is not a far walk home and I don't want to be near the other kids right now. The school guard helps me cross the street. Along the way, I pass the park. I wish I could stop there, but I know I can't. Mama will be worried if I don't come home right away. Daddy will be mad. Maybe Ash will come over today. Maybe he will tell me another story. Today, during lunch and recess at school, I wrote out the stories he'd told me. I also wrote about last night. That was tough. One of my teachers asked me what I was writing—I just told her it was a story. She let it go at that. I was glad. I was afraid she might ask me to read it. That would be awful. But the more I write in my story notebooks, the more I love them. I love to write things, and I love to read them even more.

I don't feel so dumb anymore. Maybe I'm not dumb. After all, I am sure that Ash would not be my friend if I were. He says he thinks I'm pretty smart. He says I have a real talent for writing, too. He wants me to show one of my writings to my teacher. I don't think I could do that, though. I sure hope he comes over today. Or maybe I could walk back to the park, later, before dinner, and he'd be there.

There's home, the red brick, two-story house that I've always lived in. Mama doesn't like its black shutters— she wants them to be white. She's always wanted them to be white. Daddy keeps saying he'll paint them. But he never does. I don't know why. Sometimes when I hear him say that, I think that I should find the paint myself in the basement and paint them for her. But I know that I can't really do that. I'm just a kid. The one thing I like most about our house, besides the backyard and its maple tree, is the mailbox. It's stone and big. It reminds me of what a mailbox at a castle might look like. It's my job to get the mail every day when I get home from school, since I walk right past it to the front door. We never get anything but bills, so I don't know why Mama and Daddy even care. But, just like I'm s'posed to, I stop and pull out two white envelopes addressed to my Daddy. Then I head on into the house.

Usually, Mama's in the kitchen, starting on supper. Usually, when I come in, I can hear the TV on in the living room where Daddy's watching a game or the news or something. Usually, there's some kind of noise. But today there is not. Mama's not in the kitchen. I don't see any pots or anything on the stove. I don't hear the TV on either. Frowning, I put my bookbag on the floor by the front door and start walking towards the kitchen.

"Mama!" I call.

No answer.

"Daddy?"

"We're in here, sweetie," Mama says from upstairs.

That's weird, I think, but start up the stairs anyway. As I get to the top of the stairs, I can see my dad's foot in the bonus room. He's laying on the floor. Then he laughs.

I walk in and what I see I cannot believe.

Mama is sitting on the couch and at her feet is a little puppy. He's yellow and perfect. He has a shiny black nose and beautiful ears. He is running back and forth between my mom and dad. Daddy sits up and he is grinning broadly.

"Hey, peaches. Remember how you said you wanted a dog? How's this one?"

"Really? Really, I can keep him?" I ask, running and sitting down in front of the door.

I pat the floor to try and get him to come to me. He does, and I cup his furry face and start to pet him. I love him already.

"You can keep him, but you have to help me train him and clean up after him," Mama says, raising her brows.

"Sure, sure! Oh, thank you!"

"You need to thank your daddy: he's the one who got you the dog."

Suddenly, I'm not as excited.

I look at my dad and he smiles at me, winks a little.

"You've been such a good girl, I thought it was time you got something special, something just as special as you are."

I try hard to smile but all I can manage is a small one, and it's shaky. I look back down at the dog.

"Thank you," I mutter.

Daddy reaches out and squeezes my neck. I feel my muscles go hard and then I force them to relax. Everything is okay. Mama is here.

"Well, I better go ahead and start on supper. The dog's bowl and food and stuff are in the kitchen, Anna. You bring him on down when you're ready to feed him."

My mom starts to stand. I look at her and then back down at the dog. I pet him again and pick him up to hold him close to me.

"What are you going to name him?" Daddy asks, moving to sit up now, too.

I shrug.

"Well, he seems to be a really playful pup. Guess you'll just have to watch him for a little while until you think of something that fits him."

I nod once.

"May I take him outside?"

"Sure. Probably a good idea."

Daddy stands and sits down on the beige couch, grabbing the remote to the small TV that sits in the room.

As I walk downstairs, holding my new puppy, I try to be happy. I *have* wanted a dog for a really long time. And this one *is* perfect. I love his yellow, golden color. I love the playfulness. I love everything about the dog. Everything except that I know why I got him. I got him cause I was "good" last night and cause I didn't tell today. Daddy always does this: he buys me stuff. It's always good stuff, and a lot of times it's stuff that I've really wanted or asked for. But whenever I get it, 'specially if it's real close to when he came to my room, I feel bad. I don't know why. I don't know why it bothers me. But it does. It really does.

8
The Discovery

"Can you tell me a story?"

One of Ash's dark eyebrows lifted. He crossed both arms over his chest and seemed to think about the question. Finally, he tipped his head down and looked at me.

"I don't rightly know. What kind of story would you like to hear?"

"A new one! Tell me something true. Nothing about blue crickets sneaking into the queen's shoe this time," I insisted, feeling my nose crinkle slightly.

I love Ash. He's been my friend for a really long time. Like, since my birthday, and that was almost a whole year ago. He is the coolest storyteller ever, mainly cause he knows tons of them. He's been all over the world, and he tells me stories about the places he's been. Sometimes he even brings me little trinkets to look at, brought back from faraway places, like Alaska and New York. And one time he even showed me a picture of a real lady from India. I could listen to Ash's stories all day. Mostly, though, I love Ash cause...well, cause he's nice. Even if sometimes he's a little weird, like when he tells me stories about blue crickets (I don't think there really are such things) that get into the queen's shoes and he tries to make me believe it really happened. I might be only ten, but, really, I know better.

"How bout you tell me a story first?" he asked, leaning back against the maple tree in my backyard.

"I don't know any stories," I said.

"Well—"

"Anna!"

The sound of my daddy calling me made my head jerk towards our back door. He sounded a little mad. I started scrambling to my feet, grabbing my notebook with one hand. Then I looked back at Ash, who was still sitting against the maple tree.

"I gotta go," I said, feeling my hand clench and unclench. I couldn't keep from looking over my shoulder towards the door again, either. My dad wouldn't wait for long.

Ash inclined his head. "You gotta go," he repeated slowly and quietly.

"Bye," I said and turned to go.

"Anna?"

Ash's voice stopped me. Frowning, I looked over my shoulder at him. For a long moment, he said nothing but then, finally, he said what he always says to me before he goes away. "Écrivez-moi." I usually smile when he says this but, right now, I'm in a hurry. He seems to know this cause he winks at me and then nods towards the door. I turn and run but when I get to the steps of our back porch, I look over my shoulder to see him. Ash still sits at the maple tree and he is watching me. He winks at me.

***** ***** *****

The ceiling above my bed slants down. Almost right in the center of the portion above my head is a crack. It's not a very big crack, and Mama always says she needs to fix it, but I kind of like it. It reminds me of me. Daddy's hands are smooth. They don't look nothing like Ash's hands, which have big sores on them and feel kind of rough. I like Ash's hands, even though they remind me of sandpaper. Daddy's hands are not rough at all. They're smooth. And clean, too. He smells of cedar wood, cause he's been in the basement all day making benches. He's

120

real good at that sort of thing—making wood into real things that we can use. I used to wonder how his hands could stay so smooth and clean when he worked with wood. He says it's so that he can be "easy with me." I don't really know what that means, but I think I kind of do. Whenever he says he's gotta be "easy with his girl," it makes me sad. I—

"Aaaah."

Without meaning to, a little cry comes out of me as my body jerks. I hate this part the most, when the hard thing sticks me. Most of the rest of it, I just kind of watch from above. Sometimes I cry, but that just makes it all the worse. Most of the time, I don't need to cry anyway cause it don't really hurt that bad no more. Except for the sticking part. That hurts and it's hard not to cry out even though I try to be a "big girl" like Daddy tells me I should be. It gets really hard to think after the sticking part for a few minutes cause it just keeps going on and on and on. I hear the sound of the bed creaking when Daddy reaches above me and grabs the headboard. I try to turn my head sideways, but it's really hard to do cause Daddy's chest is in my face. The hairs on his chest are really prickly. Finally, it's still. Daddy falls on top of me and makes a deep rumble. Then the hard thing falls out. It is easier to think again now.

Daddy stands up and walks over to the dresser. He pulls out a cigarette and sits down on the chair beside the night table. I look away, first at the door to my room, then down at the sheets where I see my hands and realize they are clutching the sheet. I stare at them for a long time, until the sound of Daddy's voice jerks me.

"Were you talkin' to Ash?"

I can't talk. I have to answer him but I suddenly realize that my teeth are ground so hard against each other that I can't unlock my jaw. I squint my eyes and try really hard. Finally, my teeth unclamp.

121

"Yes, sir," I answer.

"Your teacher said he came to eat lunch with you at school."

I nod.

"You know your mother doesn't like you talkin' to Ash."

This time, I say nothing. I can't stop being friends with Ash. That would be, like, totally the worst thing in the world. But all I say is, "Yes, sir."

Daddy grabs his pants and heads towards the door. As he opens it, he says, "Get dressed."

And me: "Yes, sir."

My eyes are back, now, on the crack in the ceiling above my head. I wonder if the roof hurt when the crack formed. I do like that crack. It and me are a lot alike.

***** ***** *****

It hurts to walk. It hurts in my private part and it also hurts in my right leg. It makes me walk a little funny, but I still walk as fast as I can outside. I hope Ash is there. When I get outside, though, he's not there. It's just the maple tree. I go and sit beneath it. When I sit down, I can feel the blades of grass poking me. Most of the time, I like this feeling cause it's a soft prickly, but right after Daddy comes to my room I don't like it much. It reminds me of the prickly hairs and the rough skin of his legs. But it's okay cause I have pants on now. And my flashlight so that I can see in the dark. I prop the flashlight up on a stump to the side of me and lay down on my belly in the grass so that the light shines on the notebook. When I open it up, I have just enough light, from the flashlight and the moon, to see enough to write. I don't know why I do it, but after Daddy leaves I usually have to write about it. If I don't, I start feeling like I can't breathe and it's hard to think, especially

122

in school. It's kind of like my way of remembering so I can forget cause once I write about it, I try real hard not to think about it again. Ever. It don't always work that good but then it does work a lot of times, too.

Three pages have been written when I see the first tear hit the page. It makes a round dot and the words that I have just written smear, the blue ink turning darker. That makes me sad, too. How stupid of me not to wipe my eyes in time. Suddenly, there are more tears. They are salty as they slip into the corner of my mouth. I grab the edge of my blue sweater with my fingers and pull the edge of my sleeve up into my palm, and then I use that to wipe my face.

"Do you still want to hear a true story?"

Ash's voice is so deep. When my mama hears somebody talk like Ash, she says it sounds "rich as molasses." I like that cause molasses is sweet and so is Ash. Just hearing his voice makes me instantly happy. I scramble to sit up while Ash watches me and lowers himself to the ground. I did not hear him come in. But that's like a lot of times. He's real quiet. I don't think nothing about it when he takes my notebook and puts it behind him so that he can sit closer to me.

"Hi, Ash," I say, wiping the last of my tears away.

"Hi. You okay?"

I nod.

"I want to hear a story."

"C'mere, and I'll tell you one."

He opens his arms and I move closer to his side. Ash's hugs are the best. And I love it especially much when he lets me sit real close to him like this while he tells me a story.

"What's this story about, Ash?"

"Once upon a time, in a land far away, there lived a little boy. He liked lots of things. He liked playing baseball.

123

He liked spaghetti. He liked video games, especially Mario. He also loved cars. His favorite kind were the red sports cars. He had a ton of them to play with, and whenever his birthday or Christmas came around, he always asked for a different version of the same thing: a red car. This little boy even liked school. But there was one thing he did not like."

"What was that?"

"Change. He hated change. After the last snow melted and the weather started turning warmer, his mother would do 'spring cleaning.' He hated this, cause she always moved things around the house. One time, she moved the coffee table to a different place and when the boy went to set his drink down on the table to watch TV, it dropped onto the floor cause the coffee table wasn't where it was supposed to be. He could never find anything he needed cause his mother would always 'put it away' for him— except she put it in a different spot every time! Whenever a new school year started, he had to get a new teacher. He didn't like that cause he never knew if the new teacher was going to be as good or worse than the teacher the year before. If his mother made a meal different than she usually did, he wouldn't eat it. Everything had to stay exactly the same. Well, one day, his mommy and his daddy told him something bad. Real bad. They told him that they were going to be moving. Moving, d'ya hear?! The boy had been *born* in the house he lived in. I mean, really *born* in it: his mommy hadn't gone to a hospital like most mommies did. The boy cried and cried and cried and cried and *cried*. I mean, really, Anna, he was very upset. He didn't know what he was going to do, but he just couldn't stand the idea of changing houses and changing schools and changing friends—all at the same time!"

I tipped my head back to see Ash's tanned, square face. His deep blue eyes shone as he looked at me. I

wrapped my arms around his waist and squeezed hard. I
knew that the little boy in the story was really Ash.

"What happened?"

"Well, the day before they had to leave his house
and go to a new house and a new town, his mommy came
in to talk to him. She sat him down on the bed and she said,
'You don't want things to change. I know that. Change is
just another word for courage. Every time you go through a
change strong, God drops a little more courage into your
courage bucket.' 'Where's the courage bucket?' 'It's in
your heart,' said his mommy. 'And,' said his mommy,
'when your courage bucket gets full, you get a special
surprise. It's very special. It's something called pride.
When your courage bucket gets full, God will touch your
heart and make you feel proud of yourself. That's a really
big reward. Feeling proud of yourself can really make you
happy and strong.' 'What do you have to do to get God to
give you more courage for the courage bucket?' asked the
boy. 'Well, whenever there's a possibility of change, you
just say okay I can do this, and I think it's going to be a
good thing and you always try to make things good. That
gets you more courage.'"

"Did the boy want the courage?"

"Well, the boy had told his mommy and daddy that
he was going to hide away from them so that they couldn't
make him go to the new place. But he wanted God to give
him more courage, too. He wasn't sure if he'd ever felt
proud. He knew that sometimes things were scary but that
he was really safe. He had his mommy, after all. And he
had God, too. What could happen by being brave? So when
the time came, the boy crawled into the car and looked out
the window at his house. He cried, but just a little, and then
he decided that he was going to see how many new friends
he could make before the end of the day. That meant he had
to go out and introduce himself to kids he didn't know. It

125

was real scary. But he did it. And pretty soon, what his mommy said really did come true: he started smiling."

"Why was he smiling?" I asked.

"Cause he was happy."

"About finding the new friends?"

"No. He was happy with himself. He felt proud cause he had done something he didn't think he could do. He was happy cause he felt special. And he learned a few things, too. He learned there were friends everywhere he was: all he had to do was meet them. He learned that doing something new was scary but it wasn't impossible. And he learned that God gives him courage so that he can feel proud of himself. Change was really a good thing, not a bad thing. It was just hard to actually decide to do something hard."

"I like that story."

"Good."

I sat there for a few more minutes. The crickets were chirping really loudly and I was starting to get a little bit cold.

"I'm glad you came back."

"Of course."

"I think I'll write that story down so I can read it again later."

"Okay."

Suddenly, we saw the light of my bedroom flip on from inside the house. Daddy was looking for me.

"I better go inside."

I reached over to grab my story notebook and then I stood. I was excited about going back to my room and writing the story down that Ash told me. Sometimes I did that: I wrote down the different stories. I had whole notebooks filled with the stories Ash had told me. Mama and my teachers were worried cause I was writing all the time, and cause they'd heard me talk to Ash. But reading

126

the stories Ash told me when he wasn't there made me happy, and they made it easier for me to think about stuff other than my dad.

"Bye Ash!"

***** ***** *****

When I walked in my room, I was horrified to see Daddy sitting at my desk. He had one of my story notebooks in his hand. His round face was red and he looked really mad. I bet he was cause of all the things that I'd written in those story notebooks.

"This is what you've been writing?" he demanded, waving one of the notebooks around.

My eyes followed the black and white story notebook with the words "Composition Notebook: Private" written on the front of it. It was just a short black square pad of paper—but it was really important to me. The memories of what happened with Daddy were in there. And so were lots of stories that Ash told me. I felt my legs start to shake and then my arms and then my whole body stood quivering while Daddy jerked open the drawer to my desk.

"Where are the other notebooks?"

I couldn't answer him cause I was shaking. And I did not want to give him the other story notebooks. There were lots of them, anyway.

"Anna! Answer me! Where are the other books?"

"The only ones are the ones in the desk."

Daddy turned and stooped until his face was real close to mine. I felt heat flood my cheeks instantly. The shaking got lots worse and I had to clench my hands into balls at my side.

"The next time you lie to me, young lady, I will blister you, do you understand me?"

"Ye—yes, sir."

"Where are the other books?"

I stood still.

"Anna!"

The voice was so loud I jumped and started walking towards my closet. Tears were flowing freely from my eyes now. He was going to throw my story notebooks away. He was going to throw my story notebooks away. But I had no courage. I didn't want the sticking part again. I didn't want him to take my clothes off again. And he would, he would do that, if I didn't give him my story notebooks. And so I gave them to him.

He took them and stalked out of my room. I wondered where he was going with them. I tried to think of all the stories that I'd written in them, all the memories, but I couldn't think of a single one. All I could think of was Ash. I wish he were here. He would know what to do. He would be brave.

The sound of the back door slamming shut made me blink. I stood up and walked to the window of my room, trying to see if I could see anything. At first, I couldn't. But then I saw Daddy throw something into the big trash can. A minute later, bright orange flames leaped upwards out of the trash can. Daddy turned around and grabbed one of the story notebooks. I knew he was going to throw it into the fire and, before I could stop myself, I started banging on the window of my room. I banged so loud I thought I'd break the glass.

Daddy turned around and looked upwards at my window. There was a funny look on his face, one I'd never seen before.

I shot out of my room, fast as my legs could carry me, my heart racing, screaming "Daddy!" and "Please don't! Please Daddy!" as loud as I could. I charged through the back door—and I didn't see Daddy. What I did see was Ash standing beside the trash can, and in his hands were

128

my story notebooks. I could hear Daddy around the side of the house. I didn't know what he was doing. All I cared about were my story notebooks.

"Ash! Did he—my —"

"They're okay, Anna."

Ash knelt to the ground and put his hands on my shoulders.

"They are okay. He didn't throw them in the fire. He just wanted you to think he had."

"Can I have them?"

Ash looked at me strangely and then stood up.

"Anna, can I have them for awhile?"

"No. I need them. They're mine and I—"

"Let me borrow them. You'll get them back. I promise."

"But—"

He bent over and looked at me. His eyes were dark, and they looked so gentle. I loved his face so much. I almost lost all of his stories. I almost lost all of the memories of the other things I'd written down, that I didn't want to remember no more.

"Anna, get in here."

My dad's voice was real low and quiet. He meant business. I suddenly knew what he was doing at the side of the house. He'd gone into the garage, where he kept The Rod: a long, rectangular piece of wood with two holes drilled in the middle of it. I was going to be spanked now. I was stupid for leaving the story notebooks where he could find them. I needed to be spanked. I looked at Ash again.

"He's gonna see you, Ash."

"Let me take the story notebooks. You'll get them back," he said.

Ash cupped the side of my cheek with his palm. His hand felt so good over my cheek.

"I promise, Anna."

129

Tears streaked my cheeks.

"Okay," I whispered and, wanting him to go before my dad could see him, I turned and walked towards the garage.

***** ***** ******

Ms. Sarah lifted her brows and looked down at the story notebook she held in her hand. Then she looked back at me. Ever since my mom found the story notebooks the night after Ash somehow kept the writings from being burned, I had started seeing Ms. Sarah. She was a nice lady. She told me I was real brave for leaving the story notebooks in my mom's car. I don't remember doing that. All I remember is letting Ash hold them for me while I went to the garage. I remember afterward, when I lay on the cold garage concrete while Daddy hurt me again. But that's all. I don't really know if Ash put the story notebooks in my mom's car, or if I did. All I know is that she found them there, and she read them. She asked me if the things I'd written about nights when the sticking part came were true. Ash sat beside me and squeezed my hand. I knew he wanted me to get courage. I told her it was true, but I don't know how I did that. It just came out. I cried then. Mama cried, too. Then she said it was over, that it wouldn't happen again. And I started seeing Ms. Sarah. Ms. Sarah wanted to read the story notebooks. But Mama promised me that no one would read them until I wanted them to. I didn't know Ms. Sarah, so I didn't want her to read them. The stories were okay but I didn't want anyone to ever read about or know about the memories of Daddy. But then, one day, I just decided that I wanted to be brave again and I told Ms. Sarah she could read them cause she said that reading them might help her help me stop having nightmares. I don't want to have any nightmares ever again. Not even one.

"Thank you for letting me read these, Anna," Ms. Sarah said, reaching over and giving them back to me.

I took them and held them close to me. I was glad to get them back. Ms. Sarah had had them for a whole week.

"Ash sounds nice."

I nodded. I didn't want to talk about Ash. I hadn't seen him since that night. I didn't know why he didn't come around anymore. Everything else is going better. Most days, I don't feel like the crack in the ceiling anymore. And there's this new girl at my school who's real nice. She likes to read, like me. One day, she let me borrow this book called *Island of the Blue Dolphin*. It was really good and so I let her borrow one of my *Baby-Sitters Club* books about Stacy having a crush on her teacher cause Erika has a crush on our gym teacher. It feels good to have a friend, one that is my age and a girl, too. I've never had a friend that was a girl like me before.

Daddy was gone. Mama said they put him in jail, and that even when he gets out he won't be able to be alone with me again. I don't know what I'm supposed to feel about that, and it's hard to believe sometimes, but I hope it's true. If the nightmares would go away, and if I could stop shaking a lot, I'd be real good. Ms. Sarah says I have trust issues that I have to work on. But it's okay, she says, cause even some grown-ups have "issues." I think Ash would like Ms. Sarah. I wish I could tell him about her. I wish he could come tell me a story again. I miss him. So I don't want to talk about Ash.

"Well," Ms. Sarah says, smiling. "That's enough for today. We'll talk more next week."

I nod, say goodbye, and walk out of the den. It makes me nervous to have Mama drive me to Ms. Sarah's, cause I don't want her to overhear stuff that might make

131

her feel bad. Mama has to go see some doctor now, too, cause of me. So, instead, Ms. Sarah comes to my house and Mama stays upstairs while me and Ms. Sarah talk. Mama says it's real nice of Ms. Sarah to do it this way for a little while, until I feel better about an office. I always have to go get Mama to tell her we're done talking and she comes down to see Ms. Sarah out. Usually, I go to my room. But not today. Today, I decide to go outside. I grab a new story notebook, in which I've been writing a story about a blue cricket who gets inside the queen's shoes, cause I can't think of anything else (and cause I miss Ash), and walk out the back door. Nearly as soon as I do, I feel my heart leap into my throat.

One of Ash's shoulders leans now against my maple tree, his ankles crossed, his arms folded across his chest, as if he's been waiting for me. I drop the story notebook and take off running. Ash is laughing, the sound beautiful to my ears, when he picks me up and spins me around.

"Ash!" I say.

"Hi, my friend. You didn't think I'd forgotten you, did you?" he asks, setting me down again on my feet.

"Where have you been?"

He shrugged.

"You didn't need me. You don't even need me now." But then he grinned, and his grin turned into a chuckle. "But you sort of wanted me around, I think. So, here I am."

I smile so wide my face hurts. I don't really care. I'm just glad he's back.

"Come on, come on, sit down. Would you like to hear a story?"

Would I?!

The wind gently touches my cheek and blows my hair off my neck as I watch Ash tell his story. It is about a little girl who believes she can do something so outrageous

132

that everyone else laughs at her. I watch Ash's face. His ocean blue eyes sparkle when the girl in the story is happy, and they darken to a somber shade when she's not. He still uses his hands to talk, gesturing often, and he still has the same voice tones. He still has the small star-shaped birthmark near the corner of his left eye. His hands, I reach out and touch while he talks. They are still rough and calloused: secretly, I think he might be a cowboy. One day, I'm going to ask him to tell me a story about horses. But, right now, the stories are not as important to me as the storyteller. I have missed him so much.

The story is over.

"Shouldn't you get back?" Ash asks.

I frown.

"I don't want you to go away."

Ash smiles, the grin stretching slowly across his face. "Little one. Go. Write the story before you forget it."

Forget it? I've never forgotten anything Ash has ever said to me. But, obediently, I stand and get ready to leave. My feet don't want to go, though. I just want to stare at him and hear him tell me another story. He nods towards the house, where I can distantly hear Mama calling me.

"Bye, Ash."

I turn and start walking, take only two steps and then look over my shoulder again at him. He smiles and winks.

I turn again to head home.

"Anna."

Heart in my throat, I turn back to him.

"Yes?"

And what he says makes me smile, cause I know that it means he'll be back.

"Écrivez-moi."

Write me.

9
Flickers of Hope

The box isn't too heavy. I kind of like moving it. It makes me feel like I am doing something good, something to help my mom. The brown box has my name written with a pen on the outside of it. That's how I know that it goes in my room. My *new* room. Mama said the old house had too much bad stuff in it. She said it felt like we couldn't breathe too good there, and we needed a place where none of the bad stuff could get to us. That's why we're moving into the new house today.

It is a lot smaller than our old house. Our old house had three bedrooms *plus* an office. This house only has two bedrooms. It does not have an extra room. It has a living room and a kitchen, but the two are right next to each other so it's kind of like they make up one big room. There is one bedroom on the first floor and then there is a bedroom upstairs. Mama asked me which one I wanted. I really like the bedroom upstairs cause, if I look out its window, there is a huge tree whose branch I could so easily sit on and not fall. I will have to try climbing out of the window and onto the branch one day to write. Ash would think that's neat. Plus, my new room has this really big closet. Mama says it's called a walk-in. It's so big I could lay down in it and still have room! There are big mirrors, too, on the closet door. I like that cause I can make sure that there is no one else in the room with me if it gets too dark to be real sure.

Right now, the room isn't real pretty. It's got lots of these boxes. Mama and me went to the Dollar Store. The man there let us have the boxes that he didn't need no more. He said we could have as many as we wanted, cause he was just going to throw them away. We took them to pack our stuff in. Mama is real smart cause she told me to put my name on the boxes that I used to pack my stuff in. That way, she said, it would be easier to sort when we got them to the new house. And it is. I just grab a box that has my name on it and I know right where to take it. There are five boxes with my name on them sitting in the middle of my room.

My bed is in here, too, but it don't have its sheets on it or anything yet. Mama got me a new bed. She said the other one was *contaminated*. I'm not totally sure but, from the way she said it, I think that means dirty. Last night was the last night that we spent in our old house. After we got done packing all the little stuff, she took me to Linens and Things and told me to pick out any new bed covers that I wanted. I got the prettiest one ever. It is pink with white butterflies all over it. Butterflies make me think of flying away. I like them. She also got me this white sheer thing that goes over the bed. In the store, it looked like a bed for a princess. Mama called it a canopy. I like how it comes down over the bed. It makes me feel like there is a curtain hiding me when I am in bed. I like that.

I open up the box. There's lots of books in this one. I have to put them on my bookshelf. It is not new. But that is okay. It will still hold my books. I start pulling them out and putting them on the shelves. One day, when I am all grown up, I will have a bookcase that goes all the way from the ceiling to the floor. It will be really dark wood and it will be filled with books, on every shelf, too many books for anyone to ever read!

"Anna?"

Mama knocks on the door now. Used to, she would only knock every now and then. Now, she knocks all the time. She says it's important that girls have their privacy.

"Hey there. How's it comin' in here?"

I look back at the box of books. There are still a lot of books.

"Okay."

"Can I help?"

I nod.

"Sure."

Mama comes over and sits down on the floor in front of my bookshelf.

"I should help you get all these on here. We could put all your Baby-Sitter's Club books together, things like that. Would that be good?"

I nod.

"Okay."

Mama starts making piles of books in front of the bookcase. If it's a Baby-Sitter's Club book it goes in the pile right in front of her. If not, she puts it in another pile.

"So, what do you think of the new house?" she asked.

I look around at my new room again. I wish there were pictures or something on the walls. I wish I had my teddy bear, too. I wish Ash was here. But, even more than that, I am glad that we are in the new house. I like it better than the old one. My room feels different. Pretty soon, it will start to look better.

"I like it."

"Good."

She frowned and put one of the books on the shelf.

"Hey, I thought maybe tomorrow me and you could go and have a Girl's Day Out and do lots of fun stuff. After school, you know."

"Okay."

We kept putting books in the piles for a long time. I really wanted to ask her something. It was bothering me. Every time I saw her, ever since I found out that we would be moving here, I wanted to ask her. But I didn't know if I should or not. I didn't know if it would make her sad. Sometimes, she'll just start crying these days for no reason. I don't like that. And I don't want to make her cry. But the question really bothers me. When she found the story notebooks and read about what me and Daddy was doing, she told me that I could always come to her, that I could always tell her anything and that I never had to be afraid to ask her any question. I decide to ask her.

"Mama?

She looks at me. She's got really big eyes.

"Mama, will—does Daddy know where we live now?"

Mama sighed. She put the book on the shelf and smiled at me. She reached over and brushed a strand of hair off my face. Then she took one of her hands and put it over mine.

"Anna, listen to me, honey. He does not know where we live, and he won't ever find out. You don't have to think about him anymore. He is in jail. You don't have to be afraid of him anymore. He won't ever hurt you again."

I didn't think I believed her.

She didn't know Daddy.

I knew he was probably really, really mad at me. I didn't like thinking about any of it anymore. I didn't like thinking about Daddy. But it was hard not to. He hasn't been gone too long. Sometimes when I am walking outside, I think I see him standing on the road. One time, I was sure I saw him waiting for me outside the school, even though Mama told the principal, who told Mrs. Keller, not to let him near me. I still dream about him, too, but that's not as bad as it was when he first left.

I was glad that Mama said he did not know where we lived now.

That was good. And maybe things were going to be okay, just like Mama said they were. After all, it had been nearly three months already and everything was okay.

Before long, we had all the books put away on the shelf. Mama went to get the sheets and new covers and canopy for my bed. It was getting late. By the time she had my new bed all ready for me, I felt a little tired. Mama told me she was going to take a bath. Ms. Holly, the babysitter that stayed with me on the nights that Mama worked, would be here soon. The day was over.

I sat down on the bed and touched the sheer canopy with my fingers. I really liked the canopy. It was pretty and I felt hidden away behind it. That was kind of silly since anyone could see me. It was sheer. I still liked it, though. I climbed out of bed and walked over to the door. My book bag was laying beside the box of clothes I still hadn't unpacked yet. Inside the book bag was my story notebook. I took it out and grabbed a pen, too. Then I hurried back onto my bed.

I always wanted to write. I could write about the new room. I could write about the new bed. I could write about how quiet it was here. There was no noise at all. Outside this room, there wasn't a step that creaked to warn me when someone was coming. There was no crack above my bed, either. I could write about how that felt weird. I didn't know if I liked that or not. I think I kind of liked it. It was like the ceiling got patched, got new paint, just like everyone said I did.

I had lots of stuff I could write about. I opened the story notebook and stared at the white and blue lines. I wrote two words but then etched them out. I wrote two more words, but then scratched them out, too.

I looked out the window at the tree. It was a big tree. I wondered if Ash was going to come by. He said he might. But there was no Ash. I shut the story notebook and let it fall to the floor beside my bed, along with the pen. I could write tomorrow.

***** ***** *****

Today is the special Girls Day Out! I am so excited! Me and Mama haven't had a special day that was just for me and her since, well, in a long time. Lately, since Daddy had to go to jail and stuff, she's said that she doesn't feel like going anywhere. But that's getting better. She wants to take me out for a Girls Day out! I don't know what we're going to do, but it's going to be lots of fun. Some of the kids in the school talk about how they wish their mothers would leave them alone, how their mothers never let them do things by themselves. Me, I love it when my mom wants to play a game or go shopping. She's great about making time "for the priorities." That's what she calls it. I just call it fun.

I skip out of the school, looking around for Mama's car.

I don't see it.

She told me that she would pick me up today after school. Our new house is too far away from the school, and I am not allowed to walk it anymore. I have to either ride the bus or have Mama drive me. Usually, she is right on time. Usually, she is parked right outside the school doors. But not today. I hike the book bag up higher on my shoulder. I don't like having to wait. The other kids all look busy, like they know just where to go. They either are getting straight onto buses, walking on home, or getting into their family car that was waiting on them when they came out. They must be looking at me. I know I am standing out. I try to look like I know that my mom isn't here, that I just came outside cause I didn't want to be *inside.* I walk over to the hedge that runs up alongside the front door and sit on it.

A few minutes later, I see my mom's blue Toyota pull into the school. She pulls right up in front of me. She is smiling when I open my door to get in.

"Sorry I'm late, puss."

I don't say anything, just keep my head down. I get in and put my book bag in my lap, like I always do, before pulling on my seat belt.

"How was school?"

I shrug.

"So," Mama said.

She looked at me with a big smile.

"What are we going to do today? Whatever you feel like doing, that's what we'll do."

I shrug.

"I'm glad that you don't have any ideas, because I do. I made an appointment for us both to get manicures and pedicures. What do you say?"

I smile.

"Okay. That should be fun."

"We're off, then."

By the time we arrive at the salon, I am smiling. I am way more relaxed, too. Mama is cool. She's not like most moms—I think she actually hears what I say. I also think she actually cares. And she can be lots of fun to hang out with. I don't think I have ever had a pedicure, and the only manicures I've had have been the ones Mama did for me, or that I did myself.

The salon is super nice. It's got black marble cabinets where hair stuff is displayed and about a hundred different colors of nail polish, too. I wonder how people come up with so many different colors. I mean, isn't pink *pink*, even if it's a light or dark shade? And who would think to try to make a different shade of a color?

Mama looks at a *Vogue* magazine. At first, I just sit and wait for someone to call my name. But then I start to feel un-cool for not looking at the magazines, so I reach over to the table and grab the *Celebrity Weekly*. It has a picture of Penelope Cruz on the cover. She is laying on a sofa, on her back, and she's hugging a white puppy dog close to her dark head. She is very pretty. I flip the magazine open and see about a dozen more people. I stare at them.

"Perfect people don't exist. Best to remember that, especially when you're looking at magazines where the photos have been doctored to make the people look better than they do in real life," said Mama.

I look at her and nod. I close the magazine.

"What color do you think you want?" Mama asked.

Before I could answer her, a short lady with bright red hair appeared in the open doorway of the waiting area. She called both our names. She took us back into this dimly lit room where there were three huge black chairs. At the end of each chair was a tub. The chairs looked more comfortable than a lot of beds. I was impressed.

"Ooh," my mom said, sitting down in her chair.

"You two look a lot alike," the lady tells us.

Mama rolled her eyes.

"I'd love it if that were true because it'd mean I'd be young again."

The lady shakes her head and tells Mama she does look young.

Have you ever had a pedicure?

Because, if you have, you know that the water feels pretty amazing. It's all warm and bubbly. She put something in the water, too, like oil or something, and it made my feet all soft. She tells me to let them soak for a few minutes. Then she did the same thing for Mama. And then she left the room.

"Anna?"

I looked toward Mama. She was putting her finger in a bowl of green stuff that was sitting on the table between us.

"Do you know what they use this stuff for?"

I shook my head, squishing my nose. It did not look good.

"They put it on your face. Then they put a cucumber over each of your eyes. You have to stay like that for a while."

I couldn't help myself. "Why?"

"It's supposed to make you pretty."

"Does it?"

Mama smiled and lifted a shoulder.

"It didn't do me any good the couple of times I tried it. Go on, feel it."

I reached out and stuck the tip of one finger into the bowl. It felt gritty, kind of like hard sand. I could not imagine that on my face. I didn't know what to say. Before I could say anything, Mama stuck one finger into the bowl and scooped up some of the gook on her finger. Then she rubbed it on my nose! I shrieked and then laughed. I didn't really think—I just reached out, got some of it on my hand, and then put a whole lot on Mama's cheek.

"Anna!" she cried.

I started laughing cause the green stuff made Mama look really silly. Mama sighed, took her palm and started rubbing the glob that I'd put on her into her skin. Then she tried to look fancy by holding her head up high.

"Well? Am I prettier?" she asked, smiling.

I shook my head.

"I don't think it works."

Mama burst out laughing.

Much to my surprise, so did I.

In fact, by the time our pedicures were done, I'd laughed a lot. Mama said that we could go to dinner somewhere fancy. I thought that would be nice. First, she said, we needed to go home and change into a pretty dress. She also told me that she would do my hair. I felt like it was my birthday or Christmas or something, except that this was almost better cause I got to do it all with Mama. For the first time since she read the story notebooks about the things that happened with Daddy, Mama wasn't real serious. Most of the time, when I saw her, her eyes were red. That was how I knew she'd been crying. She had been crying a lot since then. But today, her eyes were not red. And she smiled a lot. And she acted silly, too.

It made me happy.

I couldn't wait for dinner at a fancy place.

***** ***** *****

I stood in front of the mirror and twirled around.

I'd decided to wear my red and white polka dot dress, the one that had the straps that criss-crossed in the back. It made me feel pretty. It made me feel grown-up. But there was one thing missing.

I turned out my light and went in search of Mama. I found her in her new bedroom. She was wearing a red dress, too. I thought it was neat how we had both chose to wear the same color.

"Hey there."

"Hi. Can I wear some make-up too?" I asked, my voice quiet.

Mama was kind of funny about make-up. I could wear it in the house but I could not wear it out of the house, not even just in the backyard. She said that make-up was for big girls and that I was not allowed to wear it out until I was sixteen. That is, like, forever away. I didn't really think she'd say yes today either, but I thought I could at least ask.

Mama turned to look at me.

She was brushing her hair. She frowned for a minute and then lifted a shoulder.

"Oh, maybe a little blush. And I guess a little eye shadow of the right color would be okay, too. Just no lipstick."

That made me very happy. I clapped my hands, I was so happy, and that made Mama laugh.

"C'mere. I'll get mine out and help you with it so it looks really nice."

Minutes later, I was sitting on the little white stool in front of her vanity. My heart felt happy. I really loved Mama.

"Okay, so here's the thing. You can choose light pink or this powder for your cheeks. What do you think?"

"Light pink."

"Me too. Can you pretend you're a fish and suck in your cheeks for me?"

I did and she put the blush on me. I felt like a real big girl getting to wear make-up, and knowing that I was going to wear it outside on a special day for me and Mama.

She was about to start putting the eye shadow on me when her cell phone rang. I hoped she wouldn't get it. But she widened her eyes at me in the mirror and turned to grab the phone. I heard her talking to someone. I knew it was the same man that she's been talking to for the last couple of weeks. He calls late at night. Sometimes I can overhear Mama talking to him on the phone. I don't know his name, but I know he's a man cause I heard Mama tell Mrs. Keller that there might still be "one good man left, after all." I didn't know why Mama wanted to be friends with a man. 'Cept for Ash, I sure didn't. But she was happy. And that made me happy.

Mama says that ease-droppin' ain't nice so I tried to look at my make-up in the mirror. I liked the way that it made my cheeks look a little rosy. I touched the tips of my fingers to the eye shadow that was waiting for Mama to come back. It was pink, too, a pretty shade. I wondered how it would look on my eyes when Mama put it on me. When I was little, I liked to play make-up and I would put it on. But I always put it on too dark. And it made Daddy come to my room. He said that if I wanted to look like a woman, then I should be taught how to act like one, too.

Suddenly, I didn't want the eye shadow anymore.

"Okay, so, are we ready for the eye shadow?"

Mama was back. She was smiling, too. But her smile now was too bright. I knew just from looking at her that something was up. I shook my head.

"I don't really want it anymore."

"Oh. Okay."

She shrugged and reached over to close the eye shadow.

"I think the blush is perfect for you. And I have some exciting news. I have a friend who is going to join us for dinner tonight. He has never been to this restaurant, and he wants to try it. What do you think?"

I shrugged and looked down at the carpet.

"His name's John."

I mumbled 'okay' but I really wished John wouldn't come. It is supposed to just be me and Mama. Then I remembered that we did go to the salon and we have spent all day together. She wouldn't have fun with me anymore if I'm not nice to her friend. So I smiled a little.

"Okay. I'm going to get my shoes."

***** ***** *****

145

The restaurant was super nice. The waiter wore black fancy pants with a white shirt that had buttons. He had a black apron on around his waist and a pencil stuck behind his ear. Some of the teachers at school did that, too—stuck a pencil behind their ear and walked around like that. I think it's funny. I liked the restaurant, too—it wasn't real bright. The ceiling was painted. It had lots of flowers on it. It was painted with really light colors, too. It looked like a museum. Except that it wasn't bright; there wasn't much light. We were seated at a big booth that looked like half of a circle. When I sat down in it, I couldn't see anybody else's table or booth. It felt like we were the only ones in the restaurant. The waiter asked me what we wanted to drink. Mama let me order my own drink. I usually don't get to do that; she usually tells people at the restaurant what I want to drink and eat. I liked that I got to order.

"Hello there. Sorry I'm a few minutes late," said a deep voice.

All men have a deep voice, I think. Ash does. Daddy does, too. Even the waiter had a deep voice. I wonder why God made men have deep voices. Mama smiles. Her eyes are really pretty when they aren't red from crying. She stands up and gives the man a hug. That's how I knew who he was before Mama points to me.

"This is Anna. Anna, this is my friend John."

John smiled at me. He had a dimple in his cheek. He looked cute. He slid into the booth next to Mama and held out his hand across the table. I shook it, looking first at Mama, who nodded.

"Hi, Anna. I've heard a lot about you. You sure are a pretty thing. Just like your mama."

"Hi."

"How old are you again?"

"Ten."

"That's right."

"John, be careful what you order because whatever you get, you have to cook."

John made a funny face: his eyebrows got closer together and he twisted his mouth up a little.

"That's what I've heard. I'm not so sure about this. Doesn't that defeat the whole purpose of eating out, if you have to cook the food yourself?"

Mama smiled again and lifted a shoulder.

"It's fun."

"I see."

He paused and then looked at me.

"So, I hear you like horses, Anna."

I nodded.

"Well, I happen to own two of my very own horses. They're not at my house. I keep them boarded at a stable, so they can have lots of run. But I can ride them whenever I want."

I looked at Mama and she nodded.

"Indeed. He's already got me on one. They're beautiful but, uh..."

"But your mama hadn't ridden a horse in a long time."

Mama shook her head.

"I fell off."

"Right into the mud puddle."

My mouth opened. I can't believe Mama fell off a horse into the mud.

"I bet you were real upset," I said.

Mama rolled her eyes.

"No. I knew when I got on I was probably going to fall off." She shrugged. "Just one of those things."

"But she told me that if you want to, you can come riding with me one day. You'd have to ride with me, at least the first time, to see how you do, but you could choose which horse we ride. It's lots of fun."

I smile.

Maybe having boy friends isn't a bad thing, after all.

***** ***** *****

It wasn't until Mama started talking to John more than she was talking to me that I thought of Ash. I hadn't thought of him all day. I hadn't seen him, either. I had been having so much fun with Mama at the salon, and when we were getting dressed up, that I didn't think about him. I didn't think about him at first at the restaurant, either. I ordered a hamburger. I was given a slab of raw meat that I had to cook myself at the table. That was crazy. But all of us were laughing. Mama said it was funny watching me and John try to use the skewers to cook our food. John's piece of chicken kept falling off the skewer. He said that was probably a good thing cause it meant it was really tender. It was a lot of fun cooking.

But then.

Well, John is super funny. He also likes to talk a lot. And he started talking to Mama and making her laugh. I was happy about this cause I like to see Mama laugh. I haven't really seen her laugh much since Daddy left. I was happy that John was making Mama laugh. But they just kept talking to each other. It kind of felt like I wasn't there sometimes. Every now and then Mama would smile at me. John would ask me if I needed help cooking my hamburger (but Mama told me I'd better say no, since he couldn't even cook his chicken without it falling all the time). They did talk to me. But only for a second, and then they would talk to each other again. It did not feel like it was a special day for me and Mama anymore, even though I really liked the restaurant.

It was while I was eating my cooked hamburger that I thought about Ash for the first time today. I wished he was here. I bet he would have made me laugh, too. I wondered what he'd say when I told him that I had to cook my own dinner. Maybe I could bring him here one day, too. Maybe he'd like that. I leaned over and quietly asked Mama for a pen. She was talking to John but opened her purse and handed me one. She never looked down at me. I uncapped the pen and started writing on my hand. I was trying to write down things that I needed to tell Ash later. Maybe I would see him tomorrow.

"Anna, are you writing on your hand?"

Mama was looking at me now.

"You know better than that. Give me the pen."

I gave her the pen. My cheeks were hot now. I bet they were turning red, too. I didn't like getting in trouble, especially when there was someone watching. But John smiled at me. He leaned across the table and lowered his voice.

"I used to draw spider webs on the backs of my hands when my mom wasn't looking."

I smiled but my stomach felt empty.

I wished we could just go home.

It was another two hours before we left the restaurant. I had never sat in a booth so long. But, on the way home, I thought it was almost worth it. I got to eat lots of chocolate for dessert, and now Mama is really happy.

I think I am, too.

10
The Three Trees

"What do you hear?"

Ash's voice jerked me back.

I opened my eyes and smiled at him. I'd been hoping he would come to the park today. I had been laying with my eyes closed for a long time. I liked the feel of the sun on my cheeks. It was hot today, even hotter when you just laid on the grass and didn't move. But it was also peaceful.

"There were birds again. I heard them. And I heard the kids over on the playground."

Ash dropped to the grass beside me.

"Have you ever wondered what it would be like to be an ant?"

I made a face and shook my head.

"No. Have you?"

He laid down on the grass, putting both arms beneath his head. He closed his dark eyes and took a deep breath.

"I like the smell of the trees here. And I can smell the flowers, too. I like red roses the best. There is something special about a rose."

I laid down next to him.

"Have you ever pretended to be an ant?" I asked.

"Of course. Lots of times," he answered very matter-of-factly, like it's something perfectly normal grown-ups do.

That makes me laugh a little cause *none* of the grown-ups I know would pretend to be an ant.

"Why?"

"Because ants are cool."

I just stared at him. Then I closed my eyes and returned to just laying on the ground, with my eyes closed, feeling the warm sun beat down on my face.

"Ants are bugs, Ash."

"Uh-huh. They are complicated bugs. They only live about forty-five days, at most sixty. But they can carry up to twenty times their size. I wish I were that strong. I bet not even Goliath could carry twenty times his size. And the way they live is fascinating—they're very clean animals."

"Clean?"

"Uh-huh. Some of the ants in a colony have the job of taking the trash out of the nest and putting it in a pile by itself so that the nest can stay clean."

"That's crazy."

"Yeah. King Solomon once said, 'Consider the way of an ant and be wise.'"

I didn't say anything for a long time.

Then I said, "Do they ever kill each other?"

"What?"

"I mean, you know, there are types of animals that will eat their babies and kill each other. My teacher said she had a gerbil that was a murderer. She said he killed his father and his brother."

"I don't think ants do that. They work in teams. Like, if an ant wanted to move, you know, something really big and heavy and he couldn't do it by himself, he'd get his brothers and friends to help him out. It would be dumb to kill your teammate. And ants are not dumb."

"Hm."

I closed my eyes again and took a deep breath. I liked feeling the air fill up my lungs. It made me feel like I was alive. Sometimes I didn't know for sure if I was or not anymore.

"I have something for you," Ash said.

151

"You do? What is it?"

My eyes opened again. I looked around but didn't see anything.

"Where is it?"

"It's hidden. Do you want it now?"

I nodded.

Ash stood up and jogged away. I watched him until I could barely see him. Wherever the surprise was, he left it a long way away. A few minutes later, though, I could see him coming back. He was carrying something big. It was colorful, too. It was—

"A kite!"

He grinned.

"I thought this would be fun for us to do today."

I just reached over and hugged him.

I love Ash.

✶✶✶✶✶ ✶✶✶✶✶ ✶✶✶✶✶

Have you ever flown a kite?

The one that Ash got for me was huge—and it was shaped like a puppy dog. The tail even wagged! I had never flown a kite. I guess it's just one of those things that Mama and Daddy never really thought about. I've done lots of other stuff, but we've never bought a kite and tried to fly it. I bet it is easy. I run ahead of Ash. I've got the kite in my hand: it is trailing along behind me. Every time I run, it lifts off the ground a little bit. That makes me excited.

"Come on, Ash!" I called.

He is way behind me. I don't know *why* he's not keeping up with me. But then, all of a sudden, here he comes: he's running now, the wind blowing his hair off his face. When I realize he's coming at me, I shriek and take off running even faster, as hard as I can run. I love this! I can feel my heart beating really fast and the wind slapping

152

my cheeks really hard. I even like feeling the ache in my legs that comes after running so hard. It feels good to run. That is, until Ash grabs me and starts spinning.

"Come on, you say?" he asked playfully. He was spinning me so fast I thought I was going to drop the kite.

"Put me down!" I shrieked.

"Come on, you say? How's this?" he asked and he started spinning around and around even faster.

I couldn't believe how fast the ground was spinning! Then he put his hands on my stomach and lifted me like an airplane above his head. The kite was still dangling from my fingers.

"Let's see if this is how you fly those things," he called and started running.

The kite pulled along behind me, lifting up some. All I could really see, though, was how fast the playground was coming up in front of me. Ash could run really, really fast. He ran until we were in the clearing again, and then he stopped and tossed me in the air. I felt myself falling and I screamed—partly for real and partly cause I couldn't believe he really threw me! He caught me, though, like a baby in his arms.

"You should see your face," he said. "I don't think it's ever been so red."

"You were running really fast!" I said, swatting him on the arm.

His arms are real hard. He says that's cause he works hard, but I don't know what he works hard *at*. I've never seen a grown-up who is so not worried about work like Ash.

"Okay, peanut, let's see about flying this thing for real. You gotta do it right, or it won't work," he warned and took the string from me.

A minute later, he got behind me. He reached out around me and put the string in front of me again.

"Okay, so what you gotta do is hold this real tight. I'll be at the other end, holding up the kite. You take off running and you'll let go of a little of the string at a time. Not all at once. Keep it tight, until the kite is in the air. Then you can let go more of the string to make it go higher."

I tried to listen. But I didn't get much of what he said because he was so close behind me. My head jerked forward. All of a sudden, he dipped his head and poked it around my shoulder. That made me flinch my head to the side, so that it was not so close to his. There was water around my brain again. I felt funny again.

"Anna?"

I felt myself frown but I couldn't get enough air to answer him.

He stepped back and then came around to the front of me.

All of a sudden, there was more air to breathe. I dragged in a deep breath and closed my eyes as I let it all go. Ash had knelt in front of me. He put a hand on my cheek.

"Anna…"

His voice was really soft. It sounded like molasses. *He knows. He knows.* Before I could think of how to stop it, tears stung the back of my eyes.

"I—I'm sorry," I said.

"I would never, ever, never…"

But I shook my head. I didn't want him to tell me that. I didn't want him to talk at all. I just wanted to fly the kite. I moved back and looked at the string. The tears wouldn't fall if he'd just get up and go back to telling me how to fly the kite.

He watched me for a long time. I didn't think he was going to do it. I thought he was going to say something else, something that would make me start to cry. But, finally, he got up. He smiled, and then he winked at me and turned. He took hold of the kite that was laying on the ground and then held it up. His smile was more real now.

"Okay, Anna, start running. Let the string go slow, though!"

So I did.

And when the wind hit me in the face again, the bad stuff went away. I heard Ash laughing, and I looked over my shoulder to see him. His face was tipped up, and he was waiting on the right wind to let go of the kite. I never knew it took two people to get a kite flying, but it made sense then. Me and Ash were a team. I couldn't fly without him, and he couldn't fly without me. We're a good team.

"Anna, stop running. Look!"

I stopped and looked back, then up. The kite was in the air! It was really high, too! I started laughing.

"Wow!"

Ash jogged up to stand beside me.

"How long will it stay up?"

Ash shrugged.

"As long as there is wind."

We stood there, flying the kite for a long time. I felt Ash put an arm around my neck. A dad and a little girl walked past us. I looked at them and just grinned. I felt proud of Ash today. I felt proud of me, too. When Ash is with me, I feel almost normal and it doesn't bother me to see normal kids. They might have their dads. But I have Ash.

***** ***** *****

"Anna?" Mrs. Keller asked.

I knew what she wanted. She probably wanted to talk to me about another test I failed. I knew I failed it. I mean, I failed all the tests. I couldn't remember taking a test for Mrs. Keller this week. But it was probably one of those pop quizzes that I hate. Mrs. Keller is my teacher for everything except math, art and music. That means she teaches me lots of things. It could be a test over any number of subjects. I lose track after about Wednesday of quizzes and tests. I pass some, but the ones I pass are mostly by luck.

I dragged my foot along the floor, hiking my book bag up higher on my left shoulder. I finally stood in front of her desk. She was looking at a piece of paper. I couldn't see what it was, but I bet it was the latest test I'd failed and had to get signed by Mama. Mama has been a lot nicer about me bringing home tests I've failed, but she still doesn't like seeing them. She says it means I'm not trying. 'Cept I *was* trying. I studied every night, and I did all my homework like I was s'posed to. I think I just freak out on tests or something. Or I'm just plain dumb. That don't mean I don't try, though. It just means I can't do it. There's a difference.

"Anna, I wanted to talk to you about the story you handed in a few months ago. The one about the tree."

My mind went blank. She wanted to talk to me about a story I wrote. If she didn't like it, I was going to cry. *Please*, I begged in my head, *please don't say anything mean about the story. Please.* Then I remembered that Ash liked it. He wouldn't have told me that it was good if it hadn't been. He wouldn't have told me that it was the one I should turn in to the teacher, if it hadn't been good. But why else would Mrs. Keller want to talk to me about the story?

I just nodded.

"Did you come up with the story by yourself?"

I nodded slowly.

"That's okay, isn't it?"

"Of course it is. That's what you're supposed to do. I just wanted to tell you that I thought it was very good. It's a sad story, though. I know that your dad doesn't live with you and your mom anymore. I wanted to let you know that if you ever feel like you need to talk, you can tell me. Mrs. Hollis is a really nice lady who likes talking to kids about things. She works at school here. I could talk to her about letting you come see her."

I shook my head, looking at the ground. There was a crack in the floor. It reminded me of the crack that used to be above my bed in our old house. I felt like that crack. When something cracks, that means it breaks apart slow. And once it's cracked, it usually can't be fixed. Whenever I talked to Ms. Sarah, that's what I thought about.

"I talk to Ms. Sarah."

"Oh, you talk to someone outside of school about things?"

I nodded.

"Good. Good. Well, there was something else I wanted to talk to you about. I really, really did like the story. There were a few things with periods and capitals and other grammar issues that I had to point out to you on it, but I gave you an A because I liked it so much. We are going to start a unit in Social Studies about families and the jobs of everyone in a family. I thought that your story would make a good introduction to that unit. How would you feel about reading your story to the class tomorrow?"

My mind sort of just froze up. All I could hear was that she liked the story and that I got an A, even though I had messed up some of the grammar stuff. Then, it was like I sort of got un-stuck. She wanted me to read the story out loud in front of the other kids. I was nervous about that. But I was happy, too. That meant that I would be a real storyteller, just like Ash. Wow.

"Would that be okay?" Mrs. Keller asked me again.

"What if they laugh at me?"

"They won't laugh at you. It's a good story, Anna."

157

I nodded and gave a little smile.

"Okay."

"Great." She smiled at me and then added, "Have a good afternoon," which reminded me that I could go. School is out.

I walked through the hallways towards the entrance of the school. There were tons of kids. They were all talking and laughing. Some of them were standing by their lockers. This was the first year we got lockers. This was also the first year that we had to "switch classes." Used to, we had the same teacher for everything. I thought it made me look more like a big kid. It made the school seem bigger, too, somehow, with kids always going somewhere.

The funny thing, though, was that I didn't hardly see the kids. I couldn't hear them either. All I could think about was Mrs. Keller. Tomorrow, she wanted me to read my tree story to the whole class. I felt like I was walking in a fog. I could not believe this! Mostly, I could not wait to tell Ash!

***** ***** *****

Mama didn't want me to stay with the babysitter anymore. She said John could watch me. He had started staying over a lot. That was okay. I liked John. He was nice to me. Tonight, he asked me if I wanted to play Scrabble. I had just started playing that game last year. I wasn't real good at it but I said sure cause it was something to do.

He set the game up in the living room, and he turned on a basketball game.

"So, how was school?"

"Good. I get to read a story I wrote to the class tomorrow."

Mama had been so proud of that. She told me that.

"That's great. I'm sure they'll love it."

He went first and made the word *swims.*

"Yeah. It's about this tree. Well, really, it's about these three trees. One of the trees is little, kind of like a baby, and the other two trees are taller. They're called the Mama and Daddy."

"Yeah? That's great."

He looked at the word I made — *win* — and frowned.

"Hm. This might take me a minute here. I don't have a whole lot of good letters."

I was still excited about getting to talk about the story. I didn't even really care about the Scrabble game.

"There's this monkey that plants all three trees. He plants the baby tree in the middle of the other trees. Then it starts raining really hard. It rains so hard that the monkey is worried about the baby tree. So he goes out and ties a stick around the baby tree. I learned that in school. One time, last year, we had to build trees, too, and our teacher told us that if you tie a stick around little trees, it will help them stay upright. That's how I knew that about the stick."

"Hm."

"Anyway, so, it's raining and raining. The two bigger trees start swaying—"

"Yes!" John shouted.

Someone on the TV screen made the ball go into the net. I stopped talking for a minute and smiled a little uncertainly. Boys always seemed to like sports. Daddy liked sports, too.

"Oh."

John looked back at the board.

"Still my go. I gotta think of a word, don't I?"

I just smiled. He didn't seem to even notice that I hadn't finished telling him about my story. I guess it wasn't all that interesting to him. He wasn't my real daddy or anything. Why would he care? He was just my mom's friend.

"Okay. Your turn."

"So we're cheering—"

I looked down at the board and heard my voice fade. The word he'd spelled was *sex*, using the last *s* from *swims*. My eyes froze on the word and I felt myself swallow hard.

"You were saying?" John asked.

But his voice had changed, and there was something different. I didn't know what. But there was something different. My head suddenly felt heavy. And my breathing was getting bad, too. It was hard to breathe all of a sudden. I felt my face flood with heat again. It seemed like I was always turning red. Those letters—*s-e-x*—were doing funny things in front of my eyes. They were getting bigger all of a sudden and kind of blurring, too. I was still staring at them when I felt his big hand on my knee.

I felt panicked.

I felt trapped.

But there wasn't anywhere for me to go.

"Did you have a word you wanted to make?" John asked, scooting the board to the side. "Let me see your letters."

He moved his hand to turn around my tiles but then his hand kept moving. It covered my chest. Instant tears sprang to the backs of my eyes, and I felt like I was on fire. I jumped up, mumbling something about going to my room now.

He laughed.

"Okay, we can do that."

That made it worse. That made the tears worse, too.

John stood up and reached out and grabbed my arm.

I could feel him pulling my hand toward his jeans. I could hear him from a far off place telling me to undo them. I don't remember obeying him. I don't remember undoing his pants. But I do remember looking at the ceiling when he pushed me down. Daddy wasn't so fast. Daddy wasn't so hard, either. That was something I could focus on, so I did. I started trying to think about how much alike or different they were. Daddy usually had stubble, so when he would kiss me, it scratched. John didn't have stubble. He didn't kiss me either. Instead, he bit the edge of my chin. It hurt, but I didn't cry. Daddy didn't hold me down, either. He would get on top of me sometimes, and he was heavy, I remember that. I remember that he was heavy. But he didn't hurt me. John's knee was pushed into my thigh, real hard. I guess he was trying to make sure I didn't move. Daddy liked that, too—he liked it best when I stayed still. They both made funny noises and breathed real heavy-like. Daddy would put his head real close to my ear and breathe in it. He used to say Mama liked that. John kept his head away from mine, but he breathed hard, too. He smelled different. I could tell that he was wearing some kind of perfume. Daddy didn't wear perfume.

I was trying to think about that when John grabbed my hips and jerked me up real fast. It was real hard. Then he pushed me back down against the floor and that really hurt. I cried out. I remember screaming but then I thought how stupid I was for that: no one could hear me. When the sticking part came, though, I couldn't help it—I screamed again. I should have known better but, for some reason, I always felt like it was going to tear me, like I was going to have a real cut on me. It was hard to think. It always got hard to think. I was crying, but that was making it harder to breathe. I felt like I was going to choke. I felt like I was going to be sick.

As soon as he got off of me, I covered my chest with my hand. I still had my shirt on, though, and he thought it was funny. He laughed. I remember that it sounded real loud, louder than it should have sounded. I started to get up. I just wanted to go to my room. I wanted

161

to hide under the pillows and covers. I would feel safe there. I moved onto my hands and knees, trying to stand up. I cried out when he grabbed my chin, real hard.

"If you tell your mother about this, I'll hurt you. Then I'll hurt her. Stupid little slut girl, do you flirt with all the grown men in your life?"

I had no idea what he was talking about. Right now, I didn't care. If he thought I was going to tell my mother about this, he was crazy. Mama cried all the time as it was. Mama had just stopped crying not long ago. I was not going to make her start crying all over again. Besides, what good would it do to tell? It was the way things were and were always going to be. I understand that now.

He let go of my chin and I quickly stood up. I was almost out of the living room when I heard him chuckle again. I didn't look back until he said, "Whad'ya know, it works." I couldn't help looking over my shoulder. His hand had a scratch mark on it. I made that. I didn't know I was making it but now that I saw it, I remembered scratching at his hands when he pushed my head down to the hard thing. Sometimes Daddy had scratch marks, too. Mama told Ms. Sarah she remembered wondering how he'd gotten scratched at night so much.

I didn't say anything. I was still trying to breathe.

"Bleeding, I mean. If ya make yourself bleed, it don't hurt. That's what my daddy told me, and he was right. I don't mind the scratch marks, hellcat that you are."

I turned and walked to my bedroom.

My knees were shaking real bad. My stomach felt queasy, too, like I was going to be sick, 'cept I knew I wasn't. I didn't really get sick anymore. Not even with Daddy. But my back hurt this time. And my legs. I looked down at my legs. There was a bright red spot on the inside of my thigh where he'd pushed his knee down the whole time. There would be a bruise there. My front side, the side

162

that Ms. Sarah said was called my *vagina*, hurt, too. That reminded me I didn't have my panties. I'd left them in the living room. No way was I going back out there.

I got me some new ones and I got me some new pajama pants. Then I went and laid down on my bed. My bed was so pretty. Its covers were new. The canopy was new. It was so pretty. It was going to be *contaminated* soon, too, just like Mama said the other one was. I rolled over and scooted as close to the wall as I could. Being squished up next to the wall made me feel safe. It made me feel like there was something there that was watching over me, holding me almost. I grabbed my extra pillow and pulled it down in front of me, hugging it, and curled my legs up tight against it. I buried my face in the pillow. It smelled real nice. It was a new pillow. I remember being excited when I picked it and the new cover out. Mama had been wrong. It hadn't been the covers or the bed that had been contaminated. What was dirty was *me*.

I was shaking again.

I'd stopped, but now it was back. The shaking started in my legs. I felt my teeth clench and I squeezed my eyes shut. They would be red in the morning.

***** ***** *****

I blew out a big breath through my lips and rolled, again, to my back. The thing is, I was a little scared to go to sleep. What if he comes in my room while I'm asleep? He's gonna be in the same house with me all night. Mama will get home about five. She'll stay up until I catch the bus at seven-thirty, and then she'll sleep all day. Until then, though, it's just me and John.

I tried real hard not to think about what had happened.

Not thinking about it was easier than thinking about it.

It was harder not to think about the things that hurt on my body, like my bottom and my back and my leg. I wished those things would stop hurting. I was really tired. I wished I could go to sleep, too. I rolled over toward the door and stared at it. Then my eyes sort of went around the room. They landed on my desk, and I saw the story notebook. Writing was better than this.

I sat up. It made me real nervous to put my feet on the floor. I wondered if there was something under the bed waiting to grab my ankles. Then I reminded myself that I was ten years old and that there are no such things as monsters. Only little babies believed in them. I stood on the floor. I tried to walk, but I ended up kind of running over to the desk. I grabbed my blue story notebook and a pen, and then ran back to the bed. It's weird how I could feel safe in one spot and no other in the room.

I laid on my stomach and opened the story notebook.

I thought of Ash. I wondered what kind of story he would tell. He says that the best kind of stories are true ones.

I started to write. This is what I wrote:

Once upon a time, there was a pretty girl. One day she went walking in the woods. She thought she could find some apples or berries to pick. She didn't have a basket, so she took the edge of her dress and held it up so that she could put stuff in it. She put the berries she picked in her dress. Then her dress got full. She started to walk home, but she had walked too far. Now she was lost. The woods were getting dark, too. It was hard to see. Suddenly, she heard something growl. In front of her was a huge bear. It raised up on its back legs. It was a mean bear, and it wanted to

164

get the girl. It wanted to eat her. The girl turned around to start running, but she couldn't because behind her was a huge lion. Its head was bent low, and it was watching her. She knew that it was going to get her, too. There was nowhere for the girl to run. She was doomed.

Sometimes when I get done writing, I go back and read it. But not this time. This time, I just closed the story notebook and let it fall to the floor beside my bed. Then I laid down again. I was really tired. Maybe I could just close my eyes for a little bit.

In front of me is Daddy. He has a bookshelf that he made for me in one hand and he is smiling. When I turn around, John is behind me. He is smiling, too. I feel like I have to choose. I have to choose which one to go to. I can't go someplace where they aren't. I have to go to either Daddy or John.

"I don't want to," I say.

"You have to" is what I hear.

My eyes pop open. It's better not to sleep. Sleep is worse than being tired all the time. It's worse than falling asleep during a math test, too. I don't want to sleep anymore. I look over at my clock. It is one in the morning. There is still a long time to go before Mama gets home. That makes me want to cry again.

***** ***** *****

I'm sitting at my desk.

I'm trying to concentrate.

We are supposed to be reading the next chapter in our history books. I'm trying. But it hurts my head right now to read. I have a really big headache. It feels like my head is going to fall off. Besides, it doesn't help me any. I finish reading a sentence and then I realize I don't even know what the sentence just said. I have to go back and re-read each sentence two times before I feel like I kind of, sort of, understand it. It's always like this. The day after is the worst. Then it gets better. Tomorrow will be a little easier to focus.

Besides, today is a good day.

In a little while, I will get to read my story to the class. Ash said that he would try to come. I don't know if he'll be able to or not, but I hope he can.I would really like to see him. I thought of him a lot last night when I was writing the story in the notebook. I wondered what he would think of it. I wondered what he would say if he knew about John. I think a lot about Ash.

But I also think about what John said. He said that if I made myself bleed, it wouldn't hurt so bad. What wouldn't hurt so bad? And how would I make myself bleed, anyway? I couldn't understand anything. And I really couldn't read right now.

I gave up and raised my hand.

"Yes, Anna?"

"Can I go to the bathroom, please?"

"May I?"

"May I go to the restroom, please?"

"Yes, of course. Come get the pass."

I was really very tired. I almost didn't even care about reading the story today. Unless Ash comes. He probably won't, though. He hasn't come to school to eat lunch with me in a long time. I don't know why he would come to listen to me read a story if he can't even come for lunch more often. I closed the bathroom stall door. It was green. It made me think of getting sick. But instead, I locked it and then I looked at the floor. I know it is cold. I know it is probably dirty, too. But I don't care.

I lowered myself to it and laid down. I can't do this for long or my teacher will come looking for me. But I just wanted to lay down for a minute. It feels kind of funny, though. I feel like I'm breaking a rule or something. And I know my teacher will start looking for me. If she thinks I'm sick, she might make me go see that lady she told me about, Mrs. Hollis. I don't want to see her anymore than I want to see Ms. Sarah.

I stood back up and tried to look normal.

Then I walked out of the stall without using the bathroom and looked at myself in the mirror. I am such a joke.

I washed my hands, just cause it let me stay in the bathroom a minute longer, and then I went back to class. It was almost time to read my story.

In fact, when I got back to class, Mrs. Keller was telling everyone to put away their books. I quickly put my book away, glad that I didn't have to read anymore about the presidents.

"Class, we are about to start a new unit in Social Studies on families. We are going to be talking a lot about the job of everyone in the family. Every member of a family has a job, even babies. What do you think your job for the family is? Now, some of you may have chores. Those chores are a part of your job, but they aren't all there is to your role as a family member. We're going to be talking a lot about that in the next few weeks.

To start this unit off, we are going to do something a little different. In just a minute, I am going to have all of you come up and sit on the rug. It is going to be like circle group. The only thing different is that I will not be the one leading the group. A few months ago, each of you had to write a story about a tree. I really enjoyed reading all of your stories. They were very good and I liked how you used your imaginations. Some of you wrote about one tree. Some of you wrote about people who used a tree in some way. Zach wrote about how trees are some animals' homes.

They were all very good stories. One story, though, was different. One story was about family, and I think it would be a good story for us to hear before we start our social studies unit on families. Anna is the one who wrote the story, and I want her to read it to you. She will sit in my chair and you will sit around her, just like you do for me. The same rules are to be followed. You have to sit up straight, you have to keep your hands in your laps, and if I see anyone using their mouths at all, that person will owe Anna a hundred write-offs. It is rude and it will not be tolerated to talk while someone is reading. Does everyone understand?"

A couple of kids nodded.

"While Anna is reading, I want you to think about your own family. I want you to think about what you think your mom and dad might do if they thought the whole family was in danger. We will discuss it later and, depending on how you all behave while Anna is reading, we might even have some sort of pop quiz. You will pay attention and be respectful."

The kids nodded again.

"Good. Okay, everyone please go have a seat on the rug. Anna, bring your story and come sit in the rocker."

She pointed to the rocking chair that was in front of everyone.

There were a lot of kids in my class. Like, twenty-five or something. A lot. And they were all sitting in a circle, looking at me. My hands were really hot and even a little sweaty. I was nervous. But Mrs. Keller told me that my story was good. Ash told me it was good, too. It didn't really matter what these kids thought.

So I held my head up and walked to sit in the rocker. The rocker was huge. It was wooden and had a red cushion for me to sit on. It made me feel really small. But important. All of the kids were being very good. They were real quiet and they were listening.

"Did you give your story a name?" Zach asked. "I gave mine a name."

I opened my mouth. My story didn't have a name.

"There will not be any questions until after the story is over," Mrs. Keller cut in, sitting down at her desk.

I like Mrs. Keller.

I looked down at the paper and started reading.

I had only read a few words when I heard the classroom door open. I looked up. A few of the kids fidgeted. I didn't care. It was Ash. I almost started crying. He winked at me and sat down in the desk that was closest to the door. He looked really big in my classroom. He wore a brown sweater that looked really soft. I just wanted to hug him. But I had already started reading. I needed to finish reading first.

I looked back down at the story and kept reading.

The longer I read, the more I got into the story. I sort of forgot about the kids. I knew they were looking at me, but I didn't really care. I really liked my story. And Ash thought it was good, too. So I knew it was. Besides, it was fun getting to read. Stories are like that—they kind of suck you in and make you forget your whole world. That's why I like them so much. I bet it's why Ash likes them so much, too.

Finally, the story was over.

The kids were still. A few of them turned to look at Mrs. Keller, who smiled.

"Now you may ask questions to Anna, if you like."

"Why did the baby tree die?" one of the kids asked.

I shrugged and looked down.

"I don't know. I just—it was just what the story was."

"You could have let the baby tree live."

"I liked it," Emily Grayson said.

Of course she would say that. She was nice.

"I thought it was a sweet story. I liked how it was a monkey who was taking care of the trees. I also think it's like a lot of moms and dads. I mean, lots of moms and dads aren't home when their kids get home from school and stuff. I think the story just says that it's hard on the kids. Harder on the kids than the parents think it is."

Emily Grayson had just given me a huge gift and she didn't even know it. I could feel my heart filling. They liked my story. It made the kids in my class think. They felt sorry for the baby tree. That was big news. That made me feel like I wrote a good story. That made me feel like I was special. They hadn't written a story that Mrs. Keller asked them to read to the whole class. For the first time in, well, forever, I was proud. I smiled so big I thought my face was going to crack. And I looked back toward Ash.

He smiled at me. Then he winked and stood. I watched him quietly leave the room, before anyone could notice him, and my smile got bigger. Ash had come to listen to me read my story aloud.

I read my story aloud.

I was a real storyteller now, too.

11
Two Truths

I have fallen off my bike so many times that when I fall off now it does not even hurt. I can even scrape my knees or my elbows and honestly not feel anything. I just get right back up on the bike and start riding again. I know I'm going to fall again at some point, but it doesn't stop me from getting back on the bike. When it snows outside, I love going out and playing in it. It is really cold and sometimes it makes my fingers burn, even when I have gloves on. It makes me feel like an Eskimo and sometimes I think my face is going to fall off. But I always go out, even when it is so cold I could get hurt. When my mom makes hot chocolate, I always take a drink of it as soon as it is ready. It always burns my tongue when I do that, and it hurts a lot. Sometimes it feels like it probably burned off the end of my tongue, and all my taste buds. But I still do it. Sometimes I wonder about these things. Sometimes I wonder why I do them. I don't understand why I don't stay inside where it is nice and warm and just watch the snow from outside the window. I don't know why I don't give up riding my bike for something that won't scrape my knees or elbows. I don't know why I drink something when I know for sure that it is going to burn me, when I could wait a few minutes until it wasn't so hot.

I guess it's because the prize is bigger than the pain. Riding my bike is fun. I like the wind in my hair. I like the feeling I get when I am able to ride it all the way to the top of the big hill outside our house, the one that is hard for me to get up on the bike. I like touching the snow. I like building snowmen, when we get enough snow. I like the way it looks when I lay down in the snow and make a snow angel. I like the second's worth of burn that I get from the hot chocolate, too. It tells me that something really good is going to happen. And the pain reminds me that I'm real. Sometimes it is easy for me to forget that.

The truth is, I'm not scared of pain. The truth is, I'm not real scared of anything. The truth is, I don't feel much. When the kids at school get real excited about something, I don't. Even on Christmas or my birthday, when the other kids at school come back talking about all the presents they got and how happy they are about them, I don't get excited. I pretend I do. I am real good at pretending. Sometimes I think I should be an actress. Ash says that I would make a real good one. The truth is, I don't care about....well, about most things. In fact, there are only two things that I care a lot about. I care about Ash and my story notebooks. Sometimes I think about when Daddy almost burned them. That makes me shake. That makes me feel real good, but in a bad way. And I care about Mama.

Mama has been the only person in my life who has always been there for me. She's always done what she told me she would do. She's always taken care of me. I don't tell her this cause I want her to think that I'm like all the other kids who are ten-years-old but, really, I don't mind her hugs. I kind of like them. It makes me feel good when she hugs me. She hugs me a lot. She always has. At least once or twice a week, she will sit down with me and help me with my homework. She says that she knows that I am trying. She says that that is all that matters. One time, my math teacher made me bring home a test that I had failed. I had really failed it: I'd made a forty something. A sixty is failing so a forty something might as well be a zero. Mama copied all of the problems on a piece of paper and told me that I was going to retake the test. She told me that the grade I made on the test at home was the grade that was important. She did not help me. She made me take it at the kitchen table. I took the test again, and I tried real hard. When Mama graded it, she said I failed, but I'd done better. Instead of a forty, I'd made a fifty something. Mama copied the problems on a clean piece of paper again. She made me take it at the kitchen table again the next day. I still failed it, even though my grade kept getting better. Mama said that that time I made a seventy something. Seventy is a D. It's not failing. I thought that was good. But Mama copied all the problems on another sheet of paper and told me I was taking the test again the third day. I did, and I tried real hard again. I wanted to make her proud. I wanted to make her happy. I wanted to prove to her that I wasn't dumb, even though I felt really dumb.

This time I made a one hundred on the test, and I didn't cheat or nothing.

I was so proud.

When Mama showed me the grade, I smiled so big my face hurt. I was even happier when Mama finally signed the math teacher's test cause she wrote at the bottom: "Anna has retaken this test and aced it. I only count the one hundred she made here." I wanted to cry. Then Mama looked at me and she said, "I know you're trying, Anna. And that's all that matters."

I love Mama.

Mama has been hurt a lot. Ever since she found out about Daddy, she's been real hurt. She's better now. She says that John makes her laugh a lot. He does, too. I know cause I hear them talking on the phone. He stays over here a lot and, when he does, I can hear her laughing at something he says. She hasn't told me this yet but I know she loves him. Ms. Sarah, the doctor that I still have to see cause of Daddy, told me that I have to learn that what I want matters too. She says that I have to learn to take care of me. She says it matters when I cry. When I am listening to her, I just try to picture Mama finding out about what John does to me sometimes. Then I stop listening to Ms. Sarah.

Besides, I'm okay.

Like I said, I don't feel things the way most people do. I don't even feel things the way I used to. Used to, it hurt real bad, what Daddy and John do to me. Now, it don't so much. Sometimes I don't even feel it. I still cry a lot. Sometimes I have really bad nightmares, too. And sometimes I still think about what he said about how making myself bleed can help. The other night, I sat in the bathtub and I stared at a razor for a really long time. I wondered what it would feel like if I were to shave my wrist instead of my legs. Every now and then, when I see a pot of water boiling, I can't help but think about how easy it would be to stick my whole hand in it. I wonder if it would make bubbles come up on my skin. But I never do it. I am a chicken. I am too scared of any new kind of pain. One day I might. For now, I just look for Ash.

He still helps me.

I like when he tells me stories.

Maybe today he will tell me a new one. He told me that he would see me at the park at noon. It is almost that time now. It is almost time to see my best friend. Even though I don't feel much, I do always get happy when I get to see Ash. I walk faster when I see the entrance to the park. I know where he will be. He will be by the ducks, and the water, the same place where we always meet up.

Sure enough, there he is. He is sitting on the bench, and he is tossing bread crumbs to the ducks. I like that about him: he likes doing the little things, like throwing bread to ducks. And hanging out with me.

"Hey, peanut," he says.

"Hi Ash."

"I was waiting on you."

I smile and sit down beside him. He hands me half a piece of bread.

"Do you have a new story for me today?"

He turns his head and winks at me. "Maybe."

We sit for a few minutes without saying anything. That is okay. I like just sitting with Ash. There isn't much about Ash that I don't like.

"I wanta walk. That cool?" he asks and I nod.

We toss the last of our bread to the ducks and stand up to start to walk. When Ash reaches toward me, I flinch. I don't mean to but, for just a second, all I see is his hand coming at my face. The last time John did that, I came out of it with a huge bruise that I had to explain to Mama. Ash frowns but then goes ahead and puts his arm around my shoulders, just like he usually does. It is comforting to have his arm around me.

We were walking along the trail that led into a huge thicket of trees. It is kind of like a forest. Sometimes we see deer hiding out along the trail. It is one of my favorite in the park.

"Ash?"

He looked down at me and raised his eyebrows. "Yes, my lady?"

"Ms. Sarah says you're not real."

He smiled. Then he looked away from me.

"Are you real?"

"Oh, yes. Of course. I'm real to Ms. Sarah too. Only she doesn't know me by Ash. She calls me something else."

"What does she call you?"

"Her muse." He wrinkled his nose and shook his head. "I like it better when you call me by my name: Ash."

"What's a muse?"

He waved a hand in the air. "A muse is something that helps you come up with things. Sometimes it helps people write songs. Sometimes it helps them sing songs. Sometimes it helps them paint or draw or sculpt. Or, in your case, write stories."

"Do you tell Ms. Sarah stories?"

He nodded slowly. "That's what I am, really. A storyteller. Sometimes kids write them down, like you do. That's my favorite," he added, winking. "Sometimes people put them in a song. Sometimes they make a picture of the stories. But they are all stories."

I didn't say anything for a long time. I wasn't sure how I felt about Ash having more friends than just me. Like always, he seemed to know what I was thinking. He gave my shoulder a little squeeze. Then he nodded towards a grassy area to the side of the trail. He wanted to stop there and rest for a few minutes. I could tell. So we turned and went to sit on the grass. "Anna?"

I looked toward him. His face was really serious. In fact, I had never seen Ash look so serious. "Anna, I have never known anyone like you. There is something special about you. One day, you are going to have a book published, there's going to be a book in a book store and it's going to have your name on it."

"You think so?"

"Absolutely."

I smiled.

Ash's smile slowly faded. He reached over and took my wrist. "I want to hear a story about you right now."

"I don't have a story to tell."

"Sure you do."

I really didn't know what to say. But then, all of a sudden, I just started talking.

"Once upon a time, there was a bird. The bird was real small. She couldn't fly real good. The mother bird tried and tried to teach the baby bird how to fly, but every time, the baby bird would fall. The mama bird would have to keep the baby bird from hitting the ground. The baby bird didn't know anyone else. She didn't have any other bird friends cause she never left the nest. She wanted to. She would look at the trees around her. She would look at the sky and think, 'I can do it. I can do it.' And she would ask the mother bird to help her learn to fly again. The mother bird would show the baby bird how to do it again and the baby bird would try. But she would always fall. She never could do it. One day, the mother bird left the nest. She would be gone a long time. She had to find food for the baby bird. The baby bird sat in the nest and watched the other birds fly around. It watched the other animals on the ground and it watched as the squirrels climbed the trees and then climbed back down, in search of food." I stopped talking for a minute. I swallowed hard. Ash smiled at me. He reached over and touched my knee. I liked the feel of his hand. I kept telling the story cause I knew Ash loves stories and would want to hear the rest of it. "While the mama was gone looking for food, there was a really big bird. The big bird flew into the nest with the baby bird. It was mean. It started pecking at the baby bird. The baby bird tried to get away, but it couldn't go far enough. It almost fell out of the nest. The big bird was trying to make it fall out. It wanted the nest to be its home. It really hurt the baby bird every time the other bird pecked it. It really hurt the baby bird a lot. But she couldn't do anything about it. Finally, the bigger bird pecked the baby bird over the edge of the nest. The mama wasn't there. So the baby bird fell all the way to the ground. It hurt itself real bad but it didn't die.

Soon, the mama bird came back and found the big bird in the nest. She fought it and made it fly away. Then she flew down to the ground and helped the baby bird. She kept it safe on the ground. She made the nest lower so that no other bird could hurt it. The baby bird got stronger and stronger. One day the mama bird told the baby bird to flap its wings real fast. It did---and the baby bird flew! Not very fast, and not very far, but it flew a little. The mama bird was so proud. The baby bird was proud too. It was really

178

happy. It was still afraid of the big bird, but it was happy. It didn't think that anything else bad was going to happen to it.

The baby bird didn't leave its mother. They built a new nest in a different tree and stayed together. They were friends. The baby bird started making friends. But then--- one day, a big black bird came along. The black bird was more mean than the first big bird, the one that made the baby bird fall out of its nest. The black bird would follow the baby bird around, chasing it. It would peck it, too, and hurt it real bad. Other birds told the baby bird to tell its mama. But the baby bird was afraid. It didn't want to hurt the mama bird. And it wanted the mama bird to think that it was still happy. It was afraid. So it didn't tell. But sometimes, when the mama bird was away and the black bird came to hurt it, the baby bird couldn't help but wish..." There were tears in my eyes. I blinked, trying to keep them from falling. I hadn't cried in a long time, like a few days. But the tears were stinging my eyes, blurring everything. Ash leaned toward me, and ducked his head, trying to see my face. "What did the baby bird wish, Anna?"

I took a deep breath and shook my head. "It wished...it wished that the first big bird, the one that knocked it out of its nest, would come back cause at least that would make the black bird go away." That's when the tears started falling real hard. There were tons of them. I was making a lot of noise. I covered my nose with my hand and started to get up so that Ash didn't have to watch me cry but he took my arm and pulled me toward him. He pulled me close to him and wrapped me in a hug that was

179

not like any other hug I'd ever been given. This hug was so warm. It was a tight hug. He put one hand on the back of my head. It made me feel so safe and I hadn't felt safe in a long time. I cried cause I didn't want John to come any more. I cried cause Daddy hurt me real bad. I cried cause he didn't hurt me as bad as John does and sometimes I think it would be better if Daddy came back, so that John would go away. I cried cause it felt like there was a rock in my stomach that never went away. And I cried for the baby bird that fell out of its nest, too. I could not ever remember crying so hard. I cried so hard my body shook. I cried so hard my whole face was soaked in it, like it had been raining or something.

Ash never let me go. He pulled me so that I was sitting in his lap and he just held me. I clung to him. He was so strong. He was so big. But he was so good. He was so nice. He was so gentle. He was the only man I'd ever known who made me feel safe. I buried my face in his neck and just cried. I was getting him all wet but he didn't seem to care.

"Shh, Anna," he said softly. His voice was real quiet and real soft.

After a long time, I wasn't crying so hard anymore.

I pulled away from him. I wiped my nose with my arm.

Ash took his fingers and took hold of my chin. He carefully turned it up so that I was looking at him. He smiled. "You're going to be okay, Anna. All you have to do is ecrivez-moi."

It was a long time before I told him I needed to go home. I didn't want to leave. I wanted to always stay with him. I walked home by myself. Ash stayed behind. Maybe he went to see some other kid who was hurting. Maybe he went home. Maybe he stayed at the park. But I kept thinking about him. When I got home, I got out my story notebook and started writing. I wrote down the story about the bird, the one that made me cry so hard. I wrote about the hug that Ash gave me. The hug that I could still feel. The hug that made me feel better. As I wrote all of it down in my story notebook, I knew two things were true. The first was that Ash was right: I would be okay. And the second was that Ash *was* real.

12
A New Beginning

Ten Years Later

There were tons of people in this place.

I wouldn't have liked that so much except that I knew why these people were here, and I was happy about their reason for being here. Today was a special day. Today was an important day. It was a day ten years in the making—no, twenty years. Today was huge. Today was history in the making. I was here to see someone very special. I was here to see a friend that I didn't get to spend nearly enough time with. I missed her, but it was good that she and I didn't spend as much time together as we used to. It meant that she didn't need me as much. She could still see me, though, which meant that she either still needed me a little bit or she just plain wanted me around. I was in favor of the second idea.

I walked through the throng of people. A poster on the wall told me that she would be set up in the young adult section. That was appropriate. At first, all I could see was a line. It wasn't a huge line, but it was big enough—a line of about fifteen people or so, all standing in front of a long table. Seated at the table was a young woman with beautiful long hair and small eyes. She wasn't tiny and she wasn't large: she was healthy. And she was shining. She made my eyes water, she was so beautiful. And she was all the more beautiful because I knew what she'd gone through to get here. I knew *her* better than anyone else alive did. Better than that cool boyfriend who took her away from her jerk stepfather did. Better than her mother, who wasn't able to handle the news of a second attack upon her daughter and who struggled now with alcoholism. Better than anyone. I knew her. I knew her story.

And I loved her.

In front of her on the table were copies of a book, a book she'd titled *Ash*. It wasn't really about me. It was really about her. She'd written it over the course of many years. Then she revised it, edited it and wrote it again. All by herself. It was really a major accomplishment. She says that she didn't. She says that the story is really mine because I told her a bunch of stories. She says that all she did was write them down. But I know that the story was inside her all along, and that even if she'd never seen me she would have eventually written it down. I pushed her, though, when she was sixteen to start sending it out to publishers. She didn't want to. She didn't want other people reading her story. I told her that there were other little girls and little boys who needed to read what she had written. I told her that her story would help them. And so she went to the library and found a book with the names of a bunch of publishers. She didn't know anything about them, but she mailed the book to about a thousand of them.

The first time she got a rejection slip, I thought I'd made a terrible mistake. She was heartbroken. She didn't think her story was important. She didn't think it mattered. She thought it was ignored. She was so upset about it, and so hurt, that I didn't ask her to send it out again. But, whether she knows it or not, she is a true storyteller. And she knew that her story was a story that needed to be told. She sent it out again. And she got another rejection slip. And another. And another. And another. And another. I thought they were never going to stop. I thought they were all jerks. I couldn't understand what was wrong. Then, when she was seventeen, she got a cool boyfriend who told her that what she needed was an agent. She didn't have the money for an agent, but she tried anyway.

And now—now she was sitting behind a table with copies of a bound book. She was sitting behind a table with people in line, waiting for her autograph. Her story was being told, and people were listening.

I felt like a father. Except the lives of the kids who were my friends made me hate the term.

I stood in the back of the line. I was going to wait my turn, just like everyone else.

I wanted to watch her for a little while. I wanted to watch her enjoying her moment. This was her day.

When, finally, it was my turn, I waited for her to lift her head to see me. She did—and she grinned, the smile splitting her face. The people did not understand when she jumped up and ran around. They did not understand when she hugged me. But I held that girl and my heart burst.

There weren't words to say anymore.

But I would come to her again, when she needed me to help her write one of her stories. Or when she just needed a friend. I would be there. And she knew it. So I just winked at her and turned to leave. There was something else I needed to do here.

"I love you."

She didn't say it very loudly. It was almost a whisper. But it made me stop in my tracks and turn back to look at her. Tears shone in her eyes. I smiled.

"I love you, too, Anna."

***** ***** *****

My head was tipped back against the wall—I was sitting on the floor with my legs pulled up, elbows resting on my knees. I'd been here all day, and I was set to wait the rest of the night, too. Bookstores are funny places to be: there is a never-ending stream of people walking past aisle after aisle. Some of them just barely skim the titles of the

184

books in front of them while others make themselves comfortable, sitting down in the aisle, pulling out one book and reading its jacket, then opening it up to sample a few pages before returning it to an incorrect spot on the shelf while picking up another title with which to repeat the process. Sometimes there are as many as three or four people in one aisle. There are occasional lulls in business, like right when the store opens and just before it closes, where there aren't as many customers. Even at those times, though, there are always a few dedicated souls who get up early to buy a new book or who brave the traffic to stop by after work. The bookstore is never completely empty.

And no wonder.

I mean, within the confines of a bookstore, how many different adventures could one person go on? Check out the nonfiction section and read about a dwarf's life in the circus arena, or how about an autobiography rich with behind-the-scenes tales about Oprah Winfrey or Richard Gere? When real life gets boring, move on over to the mystery section and read about ghosts and witches and plots to kill; then take a trip over to the romance section to get all gooey-eyed over the perfect hero or the perfect date. If you're more of a hard-edged dude, check out the sci-fi section and read about vampires and flying spaceships and trips to the netherworld. While you're out here, you might as well stop by the children's section and read the nursery rhymes you grew up with; Spot the Dot is great and there are books made for every TV character imaginable, from Barney to SpongeBob. You'll be amazed at the wisdom in the Winnie-the-Pooh books, too. And when all that fails, when you think you've exhausted every aisle in the place, check out the young adult section. I'll be sitting here with my back against the wall, watching you, to see if you meet two criteria: first, are you young enough to see me; and second, do you hand-select one particular book from the other hundred sitting before you and me?

I have a real love of books. All books, really, I think, are beneficial, even if only in a vague sense. The worst book imaginable has a redeeming quality if it gets a young person to read. Books whose topics I thoroughly despise are acceptable because they often force the reader to think and to examine his own beliefs. In an age where most people are either blindly obedient or radical, exposing oneself to the ideas contained in even the most controversial of books is a good thing. Personally, I've seen the written word do incredible things. I've witnessed it act as the only harbor, the only safe anchor, in a child's life. I've seen it totally transform a parent. The written word is powerful. I accept this, and respect the power in every bound set of papers I come across. Generally, when selecting my friends, I am not choosy. A shared love of the written word will generally suffice for me. When I have something to say, I need someone with the ability to write it down to become my best friend and I usually don't think about the personality traits of said friend.

This time is different.

Unfortunately for all the hundreds of people who have walked right past me over the past two days and remained unchanged, I have a specific need this time. I have a particular book whose story I am not ready to leave. I have a specific friend I want to visit—a friend whose life I want to share with someone who may understand.

And so I wait.

In the two days I've been here, there have been five kids who have glanced at the book I can't forget. Two of those five were with friends and barely glanced at the book's jacket. One of the boys laughed at its description. The fourth looked promising, but her mother vetoed the book. The other boy picked it up but eventually chose a

186

Harry Potter, instead. None of them matched the friend I wanted and needed.

And so I wait.

I close my eyes.

I am trying to picture my friend, wondering about whether she'd laugh or cry at my predicament right now, a character without an author, when I hear someone walk in my aisle. I open my brown eyes.

He is not what I expected.

First off, he's a boy. Frankly, I expected a girl. But that's neither here nor there, I suppose. The boy hasn't noticed me yet. I am good at appearing unnoticed when I need to. It gives me the chance to observe. He is a skinny thing, lanky almost. His sandy blonde hair has not been brushed since the day he was born, most likely. I guess he's eight or nine years old, a little younger than my friend, though not by much. He walks in a peculiar fashion, his arms held tight against his sides, his head down. Perhaps that is why he hasn't noticed me. He looks almost like a human robot when he walks. I'll have to work on that. The white shirt he wears has grass stains on it, and the jeans are faded and frayed along the edges. His Nike shoes are muddy and, judging from the way he walks, at least a size smaller than his foot.

Hm.

I cock my head, watching carefully to see what he does with the books in front of him. The special one is on down—it's not right in front of him, and I wonder if he'll see it at all. He pulls out a Harry Potter one and I sigh heavily, willing him to put it away. He does and moves on. He pulls out a Magic Treehouse series and I hold my breath: it is another popular series for this age group, complete with mysterious tales and magic. Boys love treehouses, too. But this one puts the book back and bends down. I feel my breath get lodged in my throat. He'll see it.

187

I am sure of that now, as he leans without moving his feet to the left. He's almost right in front of it.

When he pulls it off the shelf, I breathe again. Now that he has it, what will he do with it? That is the real question. He turns it over to read the jacket. He whispers each word as he reads it. It takes him a bit longer to read the jacket than it did the other kids; his reading level must not be as high as theirs. My heart softens. After he reads it, he turns it over and looks at the front cover again. Then he puts it back on the shelf. That is okay. I have learned that that doesn't always mean much, with kids. He needs time to browse and wants his hands free.

"I said now."

The voice is raised slightly and when the boy's head jerks up to see, I shift only my eyes towards the male voice. A man has a woman gripped hard by the arm and pulled close to him; the woman has her head bent and tipped away from the man's body.

"All right, all right," she says. "Do you have a book picked out, Michael?"

The boy hesitates and the man shifts his weight from one foot to the other, looking over his shoulder. He wants to leave, and he wants to leave right now. I slide my eyes towards Michael. He puts down the Narnia book and grabs my special one.

I smile.

***** ***** *****

"Hey."

Three days ago, Michael left the bookstore with my book in hand. I followed him, of course, but I've stayed out of sight. He wasn't ready to see me yet. Now he is. His mom always brings him here, every Tuesday after school, for story time. He gets to hear the librarian read a book and

188

then he works on a craft. He seems to like it. He almost always chooses the book that the librarian read as the one he wants to check out. He goes home and reads it again, out loud, in front of a mirror, and then he does something very sweet. He gets out a pencil and paper and he rewrites the story. It is usually the same story as the one he's just read, only written in his words and, usually, it has a different ending. Reading and writing are hard for Michael—much harder than it was for Anna. But he, like Anna, knows the secret joy hidden between the blue lines on a piece of paper. There's something else he does on Tuesday afternoons at the library. He always brings along the copy of the special book and, while his mother browses the adult section for her own books within which she can lose herself, the boy finds a table hidden in the back of the library and he re-reads the special book, the one he has already read once from cover to cover. It is now that I find him.

He looks up and, when he sees me, he glances to the side. When he sees no one else near, he looks back at me. He says nothing. Anna said nothing the first time I spoke to her, too.

"I saw what book you're reading," I say, nodding towards it.

He looks down and shrugs.

"It's a good one."

"You've read it?"

I smile and say nothing for a moment. I pull out the chair next to his and sit down. Then I nod.

"I knew the girl who wrote it."

He frowns.

"For real?"

I smile again.

"For real."

He holds the book up.

"Like, you knew Anna? The girl in the book?"

"Hm mm. I sure did. She's very special to me."

He raises his eyebrows and looks back down at the book.

"She seems cool."

"She was. She wrote stuff down a lot."

"I like to do that, too. It's not easy though."

I shrug and look to the side.

"Well, I think sometimes the things that are not always easy are the things that mean the most to us."

"What other kinds of stuff do you like to do?"

"Me?"

Michael nodded.

I leaned back in the chair.

"I'm a storyteller. I tell stories. I know lots of them."

"Do you write any of your stories down?"

I tip my head and shake it slowly.

"I don't, no. Anna wrote the ones I told her down."

"Did you ask her to do that?"

I smile.

"No."

He looks back down at the book for a minute and then he sets it down. He leans back in his chair, and I catch how he winces when his back touches the chair back. I bet I could guess why. As that thought crosses my mind, I frown. The kids who need me the most are the kids who are hurting the most. The kids who need me the most are the ones who have nowhere else to turn. They are the ones who want to see the sunshine more than the tears and who try, harder than all the other kids combined, to climb out from under the rock they've been placed beneath. They are the ones the rest of the world doesn't want to see. They are the ones the rest of the world doesn't have time for. They are the ones the rest of the world doesn't know how to reach. They are the ones I love.

"So."

Michael picked at a hangnail on his finger before looking back up at me again.

"When do you tell your stories?"

I shrug.

"Whenever someone wants to hear them."

I lean towards him a little, with a small smile.

"Would you like to hear one of my stories?"

"Okay."

I settle back against the chair and tip my head back.

"A very long time ago, when I was a little boy, there was a huge pond in the back of my home. It was really, really old."

I lifted my head to see Michael's face. He hadn't told me his name yet, but I already knew that he knew we were friends.

"Like, I mean, older than my *grandfather*."

A small smile pulled at the corner of Michael's mouth, but he quickly pushed it down. I guess smiling wasn't for boys.

"Now, the pond was at the end of some rather slippery woods. I saw lots of neat things down by that pond."

"Was this the pond where the bear helped the deer? I already know this story. It's in Anna's book."

"No, this is not the same story. Anna is a girl. I told her stories that girls like. I don't think you're a girl. Anna never heard this—this is not Anna's story, this is your story."

Eventually, he'll ask me to tell him about Anna. When he reads the stories where she wrote me, he'll want to know more about the time I shared with Anna. This is good. I am excited about the opportunity I'll have to share her with Michael. I am excited about the opportunity to tell him about a wonderful girl who had a world of writing talent. For now, though, I am right—this is the beginning of Michael's story.

He said nothing, only looked down at the table again.

"Anyways, I snuck out sometimes in the middle of the night, too, just to go see it. I named that pond Pirate's Cove. There was a pirate ship named Bonehead that would sail into Pirate's Cove every night at midnight. Waiting up for it was like waiting up for Santa—but it was always worth the wait. Bonehead carried three pirates. One of them wore a bandana around his head and had a fake leg. He said an alligator ripped it off when he was a teenager. Another wore a patch around his eye. He said he'd lost the sight of that eye in a sword fight with a ninja."

Michael's eyes were big as saucers now. Gone was the tough boy act. This story was *his* now, alright.

"The third pirate was my favorite. He didn't wear a patch over his eye or a bandana over his head. But he was huge. I mean, massive, like a giant or something."

I stretched my arms way above my head.

"I swear, he came up taller than this. He could have reached the ceiling of this library."

Michael said nothing but continued to stare at me in wonder every time my voice raised or fell.

"He was real hairy, too, all over. His arms were as big as a log. His legs were even bigger. He had a beard, too. He was the only man I ever knew that had a beard. He was also the only captain of a pirate ship that I ever knew. His name was Duck."

For the first time since I first saw him, Michael laughed. It was a rusty laugh, the kind that, when you hear it, makes you think the person might be getting a cold or a sore throat. Me, I knew what it meant, though, because so many of my other friends, Anna included, shared the same type of laugh. It just meant that the person attached to the laugh was unaccustomed to frequent laughter. This was something else I'd have to work on with Michael.

"I don't know why you're laughing. If you ever saw Duck, you'd know that giants aren't to be laughed at. Anyway, one time, he told me that he could catch the trout that swam in Pirate's Cove without a fishing pole and without bait. He said he could do it with just his hands."

"Nobody can do that. Only bears can do that."

"Right. That's what I thought, too. So I stood up to the pirate. I told him he couldn't do it. I bet my whole week's worth of allowance that he couldn't do it. And then, one night, I waited until midnight when the Bonehead sailed into Pirate's Cove. Duck got out of the ship, laughing. I had to tip my head way back to look at him. He smiled widely, with one front tooth missing and the other gold, and rolled up the sleeves on both his arms. Then he bent down and rolled up his pant legs before he stepped into the water. 'Come on, son,' he said to me. 'What'cha waitin' on?' So I followed him in the water. And do you know what that pirate did? He leaned down, stuck his hands in the pond and—caught fish singlehandedly, without the use of bait or a pole! He caught one, threw it to the other pirates who put it away. By the time the other pirates put that fish in the bucket, Duck had caught another one with his bare hands! Pretty soon, I was catching one, too! Within minutes, we had more fish than we could ever eat! There were two full buckets of fish—real, live trout that we'd caught with our bare hands."

I sat back and shook my head.

"No one ever believed me, of course. Later on, as I watched Duck board the Bonehead and sail away, I barely believed it myself. I probably wouldn't have believed it, except in my hands was a bucket of real, live fish. I took the fish home that night and put them in the freezer. The next morning, I told my Mama I'd gone fishing."

"You didn't tell her about Duck?"

"No. She wouldn't have believed me. But that's okay. Because I knew he was real, even if no one else ever did."

Michael didn't say anything for a minute. Then he smiled. "I like that story."

"Good."

"Michael? Are you ready?"

His mother's voice was very soft as she peeked her head around the shelf to look at us. Michael nodded. His mother's head disappeared again and Michael looked at me funny.

"I gotta go."

"Okay."

"But I come here every Tuesday. Will you be here next Tuesday?"

"Sure I will."

"What's your name?"

"Ash."

"I'm Michael."

I smile.

"Are you real?"

I hesitate. "Was Duck real?"

Michael's grin is wide and even his slate blue eyes light up this time. "He sure was," he finally says.

"There you go."

"See you on Tuesday!"

Then he turns to leave. Before he takes two steps, I call his name. He pauses and looks over his shoulder at me. I think of Anna for a moment, and then I smile.

"Ecrivez-moi."

"What?"

"Write me."

According to Childhelp's national website, during the course of one year, and in the United States of America alone, 5.8 million children were involved in child abuse allegations and reports.

.

My heart is heavily burdened by the overwhelming needs of these hurting children. May this novel shine light onto the truth of their daily lives, and may it remind them that they are not forgotten.

For Reflection

The child who spends most (or all) of her time engaged in imaginative play is a smart child. The effects of imagination are as diverse as each individual child. In a healthy child, imagination can provide the foundation for confidence and success. In a child caught in the midst of abuse, imagination can provide real comfort and an escape too invaluable to convey with words. To this child, imagination can provide whatever it is that particular child needs to survive her environment, whether it is hope, friendship or laughter. It is not a cure. It does not protect the child from the emotional, physical and sexual scars of abuse, but it can provide a way for her to cope.

Anna and *The Character* were different for me as an author in every conceivable way. I've always been rather fanatical about starting with a prologue, ending with an epilogue, working from an extremely detailed outline, and writing novels in the third person. Much more importantly, the point that I usually try to make with my novels is that there are some types of pain from which we never completely heal, abuse being one of those things. *The Character* followed none of these rules: the first chapter I wrote was an event that took place right in the middle of the book, the first chapter was written last, it did not have an outline and it was told to me by Ash and Anna, who were most insistent that it be recorded in first person. It is also the shortest novel I have ever written (to date, anyway). Much more importantly, the driving reminder behind Anna's story is different, and somewhat harder to convey.

The media often portrays teenagers who have been abused as difficult teens, teens who are in trouble with their parents, teachers, even the law. We are accustomed to seeing abused children act violently toward their peers, abused teens who are addicted to one drug or the other: we're led to believe that is the abused child's reality. Unfortunately, it can be. In the novel, there were several places where Anna contemplated self-harm: this is a real, though still disguised, societal issue adolescents and teenagers suffer greatly from, and these destructive avenues do offer a welcomed numbing experience for the abused. It was tempting, as an author, to let Anna take that road to self-harm. But she chooses not to, for a deliberate and conscious reason.

The vast majority of abused children do not become belligerent teenagers. The vast majority do not become the perpetrators of mass school shootings. The vast majority do not resort to alcohol or drugs as a means of coping. No, the vast majority grow up to be intelligent, law-abiding men and women whose scars show up in subtle ways, often unnoticed except by those closest to the survivor. Living with abuse is like living with a chain around your ankle: you can still walk, talk, eat, laugh, cry and love—but without help you can only go so far.

Abuse is not an act that occurs, hurts and then disappears with the passage of time. It is like skipping rocks along the water's edge. Its effects are traumatizing, cumulative and long lasting. Survivors live, day in and day out, with silent shame that makes them feel like aliens in their own homes. They face the nighttime hours with trepidation, for terrors often await them in their dreams. Many suffer from anxiety and depression. They find it hard to trust (if one cannot trust one's guardian, then how is that person supposed to learn who they *can* trust?) and may suffer inappropriate reactions to intimacy and relationships. They are teenage and adult survivors who do the best they can with the reality that has been theirs.

197

Statistics are not behind these children. In addition to being more prone to walk the self-destructive path of addiction, children who were abused are more likely to be victimized a second, or third, time. This is the reason it was important that John be a part of Anna's life. It was not for shock factor. It was not to add drama or flair or intensity to an already painful book. It was to make readers aware of the fact that many children who are taken out of abusive homes are later victimized again. There are theories for this but my personal theory is that, by the time these children reach adulthood, they don't know any other way of living than by being abused. Abuse is normal to these survivors. It was important that John be introduced, too, because the healing pattern to abuse is that the survivor take two steps forward, only to take one step backward: it's a journey that often lasts the lifetime of the survivor.

Abuse is a shameful and painfully degrading, lifelong change in the development of a child. A wise person once said, "You are not raising a child, you are raising an adult." To this extent, when abuse is perpetrated against a child, that child carries it with her to adulthood.

But there can be hope.

And from an unexpected source: the abused child herself.

The mind is an incredible thing, and it has the capacity to provide a suffering child, and a hurting survivor, constructive ways of dealing with trauma. Psychology teaches us that there are a multitude of defense mechanisms. One of those involves channeling negative emotions into a positive outlet, like creativity. This is what Anna did. Anna's mind allowed her to see Ash, who dictated stories that she then wrote down. After a while, she didn't need Ash to tell her the stories—she became adept at doing that on her own. She still needed his friendship, though, and so he remained real to her. Her imagination

198

offered her an alternative to self-harm. The imagination of a child is limitless: she can imagine she is in a country that doesn't even exist and yet so thoroughly see it that she can describe her imaginary country in vivid detail; the little boy can feel his heart race like a stallion as he swings his pretend bat in the air and hears the imaginary crowd go wild when he hits his first home run. In the aftermath, when the pretend game is over and scary things start happening, the child is then able to conjure up images of the pretend game in which she previously participated, and is comforted.

Children are unlike adults. Their worlds do not have boundaries. Their worlds are not governed by knowing what time of day it is, or even by such irrelevant details like gravity. Their worlds are governed by an intrinsic sense of hope, which burns bright and is often resistant to even the most brutal abuse. Small things can make the flame of hope glow bright, even (and maybe especially) when it is confronted by evil: an encouraging teacher; a loving guardian; a creative outlet like writing, art, music or sports. These things strengthen the child and help guide her down the path to an eventual triumph over her past. Trust is hard to offer. Then again, so is flying. Neither, however, are impossible: one just takes patience and love; the other, belief and imagination.

The miracle of imagination is that it is offered to anyone who chooses to engage it.

"Suffer the little children unto Me," said Jesus.

He forgot no child. He gave to each a special talent or ability, be it an obvious gift of some art or a subtle one like the art of listening. I founded and taught in schools across Middle Tennessee a program called *Imaginations*, whose purpose it was to make children aware of their individual talents. At the start of this program, children were asked to name their talent. The sad truth is that most

199

replied that they did not have one. Yes they do! And it is our job as adults, as parents and teachers and Sunday School leaders, to provide them with the opportunity to discover and cultivate those talents. It is not as important as math, reading or science: it is at least three times more important! The knowledge that she is good at something, that she can create her own reality in which she is not harmed, but loved, can—and does—comfort and guide.

Sometimes our role as parent is to educate and explain; sometimes our role as parent is to discipline and teach. These are proper and good goals, ones that all parents should rightfully attend to. Sometimes, however, our role as parent is to stop and learn from the child herself. Sometimes our role as parent is to encourage their imagination, even when it may run counter to our rational brains. If my daughter tells me she has an imaginary friend, I am going to welcome that friend into our family for as long as my daughter's imagination deems it relevant, not just until I think she's too old to have a friend such as Ash.

Hope is alive in these hurting children, but hope is also what takes a harsh beating every time such a child is abused. Gradually, if left unsupported and un-encouraged, hope will be snuffed out, and unfortunate paths that lead to addiction will become even easier to follow. The good news is that it does not take much to combat the attack against hope in a child. In fact, all it takes is a willing heart—one adult who cares enough to reach out and give the time. It is my sincere desire that *The Character* provides my readers with enough incentive to slow down and pay attention to the littlest of hearts, to take a glimpse inside the child's imaginative world where hope is still alive. After all, as Anna so eloquently said, Ash is real.

If you suspect that a child or teenager is in any possible danger of abuse, please contact Childhelp at 1-800-4-A-Child or your local law enforcement agency.

The emotional, as well as physical, safety of the child(ren) in question depends on you for as Voltaire once so eloquently wrote, "evil exists when good men do nothing."

Printed in Great Britain
by Amazon